Trapped in the Middle

Trapped in the Middle

Adrianna Rose

authorHOUSE®

AuthorHouse™LLC
1663 Liberty Drive
Bloomington, IN 47403
www.authorhouse.com
Phone: 1-800-839-8640

Published by AuthorHouse   07/17/2013

ISBN: 978-1-4817-3131-7 (sc)
ISBN: 978-1-4817-3132-4 (hc)
ISBN: 978-1-4817-3130-0 (e)

Library of Congress Control Number: 2013905018

Contents

Acknowledgement vii

About the Author xi

Introduction xiii

My early beginnings 1

Coming To America 15

Reunited 21

Sponsorship 25

I Do 30

Labor Pains 35

Monroe's True Colors 40

City Hall 56

Divorce 67

Shaka 70

My True Identity 74

My First Home 76

The Pageant 78

Kendrick 82

Graduation 86

Chapel By The Sea 89

Financial Difficulties 91
Ivy Joy Rose 99
The Midnight Brawl 105
The Hearing 116

Acknowledgement

I am extremely grateful to my grandmother Eldeca Rose for the manner in which she nurtured me during infancy to young adulthood. She has impacted my life with her strength and independence. The qualities she instilled in me as a young child, prepared me for the successful tranisition from the very small village of Beterverwagting in the country side of Guyana, to the highly sophisticated fast moving pace of NYC.

I must also thank my mother Ivy Joy Rose for inheriting her easy going and peaceful demeanor, this attribute often comes in handy as an excellent tool during times of conflict and problem solving.

Kathryn the first time I met you was way back when in elementary school, and we became friends instantly there was that special connection, you were very special to me and I felt privileged to have you as my friend. Then you moved away and we lost touch with each other. A few years later we were reunited in the USA and our friendship was renewed. You introduced me to Ona and we became a tightly knit group of friends who had a whole lot of fun, being disco buddies. Thanks for the good times we shared, for all of your support and good advice and for keeping us all grounded. The best part of all of this was finding out that we are sisters, thanks to Ona she was the first person who broke the news to me.

To my best friend Ona, I will always be grateful to you for introducing me to the Steven's they were a pivotal part in my life during the time that I was in Nursing School. I also wish to thank you very much for being the first person who made me aware who my "real father" was, and I'm so sorry for not believing you when you broke the news to me. You are a very courageous person, and I will always be grateful to you.

To my cousin Linda for her role as advisor when I came to the USA, showing me the ropes, helping me to evade the immigration, and being there for Rebecca and I during the difficult times of our lives for this I will always be grateful.

On a more serious note, there are many people I would like to thank for helping me out during the most stressful time of my life. For obvious reasons all of the names in this book are fictitious. Will and Remy thanks for being there and offering me support, encouragement and sound advice. For driving me to the hospital when it was time for me to have my baby, and for helping me to remain focused during those difficult times of my life.

Thanks to all of the Doctors, Nurses, and the entire staff at the GSE&S center for the amazing support that was given to me during the time of my mother's illness. I will forever be grateful to you for your kindness and understanding.

Dari, Jessica, Elle and Nadia thanks to all of you for taking in a battered woman and her young child offering protection and encouragement, without being judgemental. Thanks for just listening and offering support, and never complaining about the inconvenience we might have caused you. When I think back on this, it's so amazing to realize that I had so many people around me who cared enough to help us out.

I will always be grateful to all of you and will never forget your kindness.

Rebecca I love you very much and I'm so proud of you. I would like to thank you for your creativity and designing abilities in making the cover of my book so unique and appropriate to the title. You are a true artist and I wish you the best of luck. You will always be my precious little bundle of joy.

Thanks to my husband Ken for putting up with me, for all of your help and for making my life easier. For going places with me when you really don't want to go, and for all of the encouragrment you offer in every decision I make and everything I do. I especially thank you for your understanding and support during this challenge, I love you very much.

Last but not least I would like to thank all of my brothers and sisters, nieces and nephews, cousins, family and friends for such a blessed and wonderful family. I would love to mention all of your names, but that in itself would be in another book. I love you all and may God continue to bless us all. If I have left anyone out who has impacted my life, it's truly unintentional, and for that I'm very sorry.

About the Author

Adrianna is a Registered Nurse, who is strong intelligent and independent. Her inner strength has been nurtured by life's experiences. It all began in a very small village named Beterverwagting on the East Coast of Demerara in Guyana South America, where she was nurtured by her grandmother Mrs. Eldeca Rose who instilled in her life's values and the importance of family cohesiveness. She is a fun loving person who enjoys large family gatherings especially around the holidays.

She is a leader and motivator who always gets things done in a timely manner. She is the go to person. Her generosity is apparent in the manner in which she extends help and encouragement to anyone whenever the need arises.

She is extremely knowledgeable, hardworking, and honest. Her disposition shines through in her profession as competent and diligent with strong clinical and technical skills. She interacts very well with both her colleagues and patients.

She is extremely dedicated and has excellent decision making abilities, and responds appropriately in all situations including emergencies. Her strong work ethics in conjunction with her easy going demeanor and pleasant interactional style has made her an outstanding gastroenterology nurse throughout her nursing career.

She is genuinely a very nice person, who posess excellent organizational skills. This quality is greatly admired and frequently complimented by her peers. One of her greatest assets is her sense of humor, she has the ability to make fun of most situations. Her level of confidence is amazing, yet she remains humble.

She is easily approachable and respects every one with whom she comes in contact, treating people the way in which she would like to be treated. She is an optimist who often finds her way out of sticky situations. She is an animal lover, and is especially fond of her grand puppy Mr. Bo Wrinkles.

Her greatest achievement in life was the birth of her only child Rebecca, and the manner in which she has successfully raised her as a single parent.

Introduction

Adrianna Rose is a nineteen year old who is leaving her little village in the country side of Guyana for the United States of America. Her wish is to get a piece of the American pie this is the opportunity of a lifetime. Her country does not have much to offer her, or any of the other young folks so many people are looking for educational and employment opportunities elsewhere. The number one choice is North America, most people are either going to the U.S. or Canada.

My first cousin Linda resides in the U.S., she's twenty one years old and has been there for one year. She's the one who has helped me to obtain a visa to enter the States. My plan is to reside with her and her sister Marissa, who just left for the States one week ago.

It was late November of 1969, one week before thanksgiving when I arrived in the United States. It was my very first time to get onto an aircraft, and I was extremely nervous. Half an hour into the flight, I threw up all over the place I didn't know that there were special bags tucked away in front of me for that purpose. We had taken off from Temehri airport in Georgetown Guyana, heading to JFK airport in New York City. It was not a straight flight our first stop was Trinidad and Tobago. All of the passengers got off the aircraft for about an hour or so, when we boarded again the vomit had been cleaned up I assumed that they made us get off the aircraft just to clean up my vomit. I was truly embarrassed. We touched down in Barbados then Martinique, before making our journey to the USA. As we approached JFK airport, I was mesmerized I couldn't believe my eyes. I looked out of the window and saw beautiful lights all over the place. It was lighted up with different colored lights I was in awe, never in my life had I seen anything like that. It was simply breath taking.

My early beginnings

I was born in Georgetown British Guyana, and grew up in a very small village called Beterverwagting also known as BV, which is located on the East Coast of Demerara. During my child hood years, I didn't have a lot of material things but there was always plenty of food to eat. My grandmother had a vegetable garden. She raised chickens, ducks, turkeys, pigs and had a very small shop, from which she sold soft drinks, bread, cakes, ice and other little necessities. The shop was so small, that the villagers nick named it fine door. Most people in the village did not have electricity as yet, there were no street lights and many of them used kerosene lamps and oil burners. At nights the streets were very dark, the only lights came from the homes of the villagers. That's the reason why I was so overwhelmed when I saw all of the beautiful bright colored lights as we hovered over JFK airport before landing. That was an unforgettable moment.

My brother Adrian and I were raised by my grandmother. My cousins Stan and Linda also lived with us for a period of time. Linda is my aunt Precious Pearl's daughter. Stan's father and my grandmother were brother and sister, and his dad's name was uncle James he was the fun uncle. Uncle James was a gold digger and his job kept him away from home for long periods of time. He brought his son Stan to live with his sister after he and his wife were separated.

Whenever he came home, he always had lots of money from his gold digger's job. He loved having good times he drank a lot and was very carefree. He had a small car and whenever he took us out for rides in his car, we always asked him to drive faster and he did. We thought that it was fun, not realizing that drunkard was putting our lives in danger. Her other brother was Joseph, he was the oldest of the three, and he was mean as hell. He didn't like me, he said that my grandmother spoilt me, he always complained about me. He also lived with my grandmother his wife left him when he was very ill and dying because he was so evil.

My grandmother nurtured him back to good health, and after he got better, he revised his will and left his house to my grandmother and his wife got nothing. After living with us for a few years he died. His body was brought home to the house for viewing then burial. That's the way it was done during that time. It was customary that everyone walk around the coffin to view the body, I refused because I was afraid of him and I thought that he would come back to haunt me. Shortly after he died we moved into his house, I was afraid of him for a long time and had many nightmares that he was coming to get me.

While I was asleep one night, Linda woke me up and said that uncle Joseph was in our bedroom. She said listen he's dragging his feet, and he's getting closer to the bed. She started screaming, she said that he was standing at the side of the bed. By now we were fighting each other to get to the far side of the bed to be further away from him. Then I started screaming very loudly, but I still didn't open my eyes I was too scared. Stan came running into our room, wondering what was happening. I told him that uncle Joseph was standing next to the bed. Stan said you fool open your eyes, it's daytime. I slowly opened my eyes and saw that the sun was already up. I thought that it was still night time and I believed that Linda had seen uncle Joseph's ghost.

Every Sunday rain or shine we all went to church my grandmother taught Sunday school. Many of the villagers showed her great respect and came to her for help and advice. She was an inspirational woman who practiced bush medicine, helping a lot of people with their ailments. I remember as a young child people came to her with open sores also called (te-te) on different parts of their bodies for help. They had previously seen doctors who couldn't help them. She picked certain tree leaves ground and mixed them up with aloe and some other ingredients which I cannot remember now, but she called it poultice. After several applications those sores were healed. She never took any money from them even when they offered to pay her. She was well known in the village and very much respected. Many of her patients were forever grateful and they kept showering her with gifts. Occasionally she took people into her home when they needed a place to stay temporarily. I never appreciated that, but there wasn't anything that I could do or even say about it.

My parents were separated and my mother worked to support us, and that was the reason why my grand-mother took my brother Adrian and I to live with her in the country. My first recollection of myself was when I was about three years old and my grandmother took Adrian and I to the village of Beterverwagting where she lived. On my first day of school, my grandmother took me to the class room and introduced me to the teacher. Her name was teacher May, as she attempted to leave I started crying really badly, I wouldn't stop I did not want to stay there. My grandmother spanked my behind in front of the entire class, and left me there. I have never forgotten that day. I came to the realization at a very young age, that my grandmother was not someone you would disrespect, she was very strict, but she was a loving and caring person. She was married to a police officer and together they had a beautiful set of identical twin girls. Their names were Precious Pearl and Ivy Joy Rose. What beautiful names, my mom was Ivy Joy. When

I was younger, at times I couldn't tell the difference between my mom and my aunt, that's how much they resembled each other. I never met my grandfather. I was told that one day, when he was on duty he was called to the scene of a fight, and when he arrived and tried to intervene, he was hit with an axe in his head. Apparently he never fully recovered from that blow, and he could no longer function normally. He was institutionalized.

Twice a year my grandmother took my brother and I on a very long train ride to visit him at the hospital. We were never allowed to go into the ward to see him. We were told that we were too young, so we sat in the lobby and waited for what seemed like eternity. It was very frightening for me waiting there, because there always seemed to have some strange looking people roaming around the grounds. As I got older I learned that my grandfather had actually lost his mind from the assault, and therefore he had to be put in a mental institution, so that is where my grandmother had been taking us twice a year for those visits. One day my grandmother received a message that my grandfather had died, and no one seemed to know when it happened or how long he had been dead. She had his body sent home for the burial. It was a closed coffin, his body had started to decay, I can still remember the stench I covered my nose. I never got to see him to this day I don't know what he looked like there were no pictures of him. My grandmother held up throughout all of this, she was so strong, I always admired her strength. She received his pension, and she managed a small store, that is how she made her living while helping to provide for us.

We attended St Mary's Ye Virgin Anglican Church and School, and every Sunday rain or shine we went to church. The church, the school and the priest's residence were located in one large compound, and in the back of that was the cemetery. Growing up we did not have running water in our home every morning all of the kids woke up very early and walked to the corner of the road with their buckets, which we filled at the pipes. We fetched buckets of water and filled up large drums. This allowed the adults to have water for the day for cooking and whatever else they needed to do, like washing clothes and cleaning. Once the drums were full, we fetched more water to bathe and get ready for school. After breakfast we headed off to school. We never complained about having to do chores it was expected of us and we did it. As I got older the chores began to increase, I had to help clean the house, I started learning how to cook around the age of ten or eleven, but simple stuff like cooking rice or making porridge. I started learning how to hand wash clothes we filled large pales with water and soaked the clothes in them. There was an apparatus called a scrubbing board it looked somewhat like a sliding board with ridges on it. One piece of clothing was placed on the scrubbing board at a time and scrubbed clean. The clothes were then placed in a clean pale of water for rinsing, then rung by hands to get out the excess water, and hung on the line to dry. That was how I grew up doing laundry. It is very difficult for me to understand why people complain about doing the laundry, when all they have to do is to put their clothes into the washing machine add detergent and they're done. They have no clue what hard work really is. Now I really appreciate the fact that I don't have to do that anymore just throw the clothes into the washer and dryer, I never ever complain about doing the laundry.

My brother was so lucky to be a boy, he did not have to do any of this because according to my grandmother boy children didn't do house work. Adrian's only responsibility was to fetch water how unfair but that's the way it was. Being a girl I was not allowed many privileges, I was sheltered not allowed to go to too many places, or do too much outside the home, unless I was chaperoned, but on the other hand, Adrian was free to roam because he was a boy. The rules were different for us because of our gender. My brother definitely had much more privileges and much less responsibilities than I did but on the flip side it made me more responsible.

I always wished that I could live with my parents. Even though my grandmother loved me I felt that she was too strict. My mom worked and lived in Georgetown, it was about half an hour's ride on the train, or twenty minutes by car, from where we lived. She worked for a Caucasian couple who lived in Bell-Air-Park. This was where the well to do lived. The husband was an architect from the U.S. his name was Carl and his wife Amanda was from the U.K. They had a black dog named Anna, and a fat black cat, which I was not very fond of. I'm not sure what my mom's work schedule was, but she visited us once a month on a Sunday. She was always dressed very nicely wearing her tightly fitted skirts and matching high heel shoes and bag. Her hair was pressed and curled, and her makeup was nicely done. She looked so pretty the villagers admired her as she walked past them. I was so proud of her and very happy when she visited. She stayed the whole day on Sunday I'd ask her not to leave but she always left, saying that she had to go back to work. That made me very sad.

As for my dad, that's another whole issue in itself. As children we were never told why our parents were separated, it was none of our business. That was not up for discussion, at least not with us kids. We did not see much of the man I called daddy either, he too visited occasionally. He visited much less than my mom did, he was a very handsome man with dark complexion, and Adrian looked just like him. For some unknown reason I never felt the same connection to him the way I did with my mom. Each time he visited, he'd spend a few hours and leave, he never had any money to give us, he was always broke. Whenever I asked him for money to buy candies he'd always say that he didn't have one cent in his pockets. I remember telling my grandmother one day after he left that I didn't want him to be my daddy anymore, she asked why I told her because he never has a cent in his pockets. She had a hearty laugh over that one, because I was still very young at that time. He was a football (soccer) player and he traveled all over the Caribbean and West Indies. Apparently he was away from home for extended periods of time, and did not live up to his obligations. My mom had no other choice but to seek employment.

She had an apartment in the city where we occasionally visited her. We traveled by train, it was cheaper to take the train than to go by a hired car. As we got older, we were allowed to take the train by ourselves. My grandmother sent us off very early to catch the train she wanted to make sure we didn't miss it. Many times we waited for an hour or more, and the station was deserted during off hours. All of the stations had homes attached to them, and each one had a station master assigned to it who lived there with his family. Each station carried the name of the village of their location and this station was named Beterverwagting Train Station.

I noticed each time I waited for the train, the station master made an effort to speak with me. He always asked where I was going, and commented on the fact that my grandmother was sending me off much too early to wait for the train. Many times he sat and chatted with me to keep me company. Whenever I attempted to purchase my ticket for the trip, he never took the money from me. As I waited for the train one day, he informed me the next local train wasn't due to arrive for a couple of hours. He said an express train was scheduled to pass by shortly, he would flag it down and when it stopped I should board the train but not let anyone know he stopped it just for me.

I asked my mom if he was related to us, I told her about his kindness and generosity, and how he always asked if I needed anything. I told her about the time he stopped the express train just for me so I wouldn't have to wait for hours before the local train was scheduled to arrive. She looked at me and smiled and said he was just a good friend. I knew they were friends because whenever my mom visited us he came by to see her.

When Adrian and I made conformation it was a great accomplishment all of the kids looked forward to the ceremonies of the day. We all wore white and received the holy communion for the first time. After the church ceremony was over, all of our family and friends came to our home for a huge celebration which my mom and grandmother planned for us. The station master was there he came with a few of his friends. From now on I'll call him Mr. B. We all had a very good time, that's one of my life long memories.

My mom's employer relocated to London and shortly after their first child was born. They offered her the nanny's job for their baby and she accepted. This was a great opportunity for her to leave the country. Her mother was doing an excellent job taking care of her two children, and she knew she would never have to worry about us. When my mom left for London, I was thirteen years old and felt very dejected. I was very sad and it showed, people always asked me why I looked so sad.

Shortly after she left, it was time for me to start high school. I attended Montmarte High in Georgetown it was a private school, which was located on South Rd, Bourda. This school was actually held in a two story house. Since the school was located in the city, I traveled by train every day. That was fun and freedom. There were kids from the entire east coast travelling to Georgetown every day on the train to go to school without any adult supervision, and that was probably the most freedom many of us had experienced so far.

My mom corresponded regularly with us we were always looking out for the mail man for overseas mail. We did not have a telephone, and of course there was no internet at that time. So things moved slowly. My mom paid my tuition, but she said that she couldn't afford to pay the cost of the monthly train fare. My grandmother did not have the means to afford that either and I dared not ask my dad, since he never had one cent in his pockets. I wrote to my mom again, and when she responded she told me that I should go to Mr. B. and ask him to pay for my monthly tickets, which we called contracts. I couldn't understand this, and frankly I was embarrassed to go and ask him for that favor. I discussed this with my grandmother, and she reminded me that without his help I wouldn't be able to attend high school. Reluctantly I informed him of my mom's suggestion of him providing my monthly contracts. He agreed without any hesitation I was relieved and thanked him very much for being so kind. Again I thought what a nice person he was.

He had seven children who always seemed to be very reserved, they never really mixed with the kids in the village, they were generally very quiet and they frequented the library. I became very close with one of his daughters, her name is Kathryn we attended the same elementary school, but I was in a higher grade than she was, since I am older, and for some unknown reason we became good friends. They left the village I believe that Mr. B was transferred to another station.

I was very quiet and reserved, and one of the teachers called me melancholy, he thought I seemed sad all of the time. I was a very good student I was third in my class. By the end of my first year of high school, I had started to loosen up as a matter of fact I became very outspoken, and joined the band wagon of the so called trouble makers of the class. With this new behavior, my grades dropped significantly. I remember once, one of the guys in my class stuck a straight pin upwards in the teacher's chair, it was just before we were to start our French period, for some reason we took a lot of foreign languages. We all sat in our seats very quietly with our books opened to the correct lesson, waiting patiently for our teacher to arrive and take his seat. When he came to the class room he couldn't believe his eyes or ears that his entire class was sitting quietly with their books opened to the correct lesson, he was smiling from ear to ear. He somehow thought that we had matured overnight. He even commented that he thought that he was in the wrong class room, and we all smiled. All eyes were on him, as soon as he sat down, he jumped up faster than he sat down and yelled out loudly as he rubbed his ass. His smile disappeared instantly, the entire class started laughing we were in an uproar, everyone was laughing and trashing around he was so mad he started to stutter. The principal came running he heard the commotion the teacher told him that one of us planted the straight pin in his seat. The principal asked us one by one who did it along with the threat of suspension every one denied doing it or even seeing who did it we were a very small and tightly knit class. I was one of the main suspects, he stared me down when he asked me, but I looked him straight in his eyes and told him that I did not see who did it. Our entire class received detention but we didn't care, because the look of confusion, anger and hurt on that teacher's face when he sat down on the straight pin was worth any detention, I'm still chuckling as I write this even though it was such a long time ago.

Another time, a few of us decided to leave the class room while classes were in session to go and ride our bikes. We rode around the block a few times and every time we passed by the school, we waved at our classmates. We were having a grand time until we saw the principal of our school on his bike riding towards us. As he got closer to us, his facial expression was full of anger and frustration. The look on his face actually scared us. We rushed back in, threw our bikes into the garage and ran back into the class room and took our seats. The other kids were really laughing at us, we were not laughing we knew that we were in big trouble. We were immediately summoned to the principal's office, where we were given a lecture on behavior and each one of us received one week's suspension. We were then informed that we could not return without a parent or guardian. I was terrified I couldn't tell my grandmother about the suspension she was so strict I knew that I would be in trouble. My punishment would have been a good ass whipping, parents or grandparents were allowed to whip asses, with no questions asked. This was looked upon as discipline and no one dared question this fact.

For the next week I got dressed for school every day and took the train to the city. I went to my aunt Precious Pearl's house and begged her not to tell my grandmother about the suspension, for some unknown reason she agreed to keep it a secret, I was very happy. So every day I stayed there, and at the end of the suspension, my aunt accompanied me back to school, she spoke with the principal on my behalf and I was accepted back into the school. I have never forgotten that great favor my aunt did for me, and remained forever thankful. I behaved after that suspension I never wanted to be in that situation again.

During my high school years, I dated a local boy from the village, his name was Marty Jones. We rode the train together he also attended high school in the city. My grandmother allowed him to visit, but we were not allowed to go out on dates. That was enough for me, because I didn't think that she would even allow me to date, so I was thankful for that. I was allowed to go to some social functions, but only the ones that were sponsored by the church school. My grandmother always showed up at the event to take me home. I was in love with Marty, and I assumed that he was in love with me at least that's what he told me. I had a very good girl friend, her name was Cheri Eason we were very close, she visited me every day after school and we hung out all of the time. People started telling me that they saw Cheri and Marty together in romantic situations. I did not believe them, but

I noticed that Cheri had stopped coming to my house after school. I confronted him and of course he denied. So to make him jealous I asked my cousin Linda to write me a love letter pretending that it was from a boy, and I placed it in one of my text books, making sure that he'd find it. We sat together on the train every day, and of course I made sure he found the letter. He read the letter and asked Linda if she knew who sent me that letter of course she denied not knowing who sent it.

Early one evening I took my little nephew Wesley for a walk we were heading towards the train station, and I saw my boyfriend with my best girlfriend standing very close and smiling in each other's face, there was no mistake what was going on. They were literally drooling over each other. I passed right next to them they saw me, but they just kept looking into each other's eyes. They acted as though I didn't exist. I couldn't believe it, I was devastated. A few days later Marty came to my home and asked me to forget whatever I had seen the other day. He insisted he was just having a friendly conversation with Cheri, and there wasn't anything going on between them. I called him a cheater and a liar, and told him to get the hell out of my house, and I never wanted to see either one of them again. I stopped speaking to both of them, I was very hurt I had many sleepless nights, I couldn't eat I had no appetite, I lost weight and that was something I couldn't afford to do since I was already too thin. All I could do was be reminiscent of our love. I kept thinking of the way we hugged and kissed, the way I felt when I was in his arms, and how much I loved him. The way he looked at me, was the exact way he was looking at that little bitch. I couldn't stand it I didn't think I would survive the break up. Shortly after he disappeared from the village I was informed he had joined the police academy and was away training in the city. I kept looking out for him every day hoping he would come by and apologize, but he never did.

His oldest sister was a hairstylist she was having a hair show and she asked me to be one of the models for her show and I accepted. After the show we were having an after party, and he showed up I believe that it was a set up between him and his sister. I was happy to see him, because deep down I was still in love with him. We started talking again, but the relationship was not as it was in the beginning. He was away in training most of the time and this limited our time together.

My mother was making plans for me to go to England after high school. Her desire was for me to attend nursing school in England. She contacted a school of nursing in Devon England I sent in all of their requirements and was accepted into their nursing program. I was very happy and excited finally I would be joining my mother again.

I went into the British embassy in Georgetown with my school's acceptance letter to apply for a student's visa. I was seventeen years old, the day of the interview I was alone and the interviewer was a son of a bitch. He asked me a bunch of questions like why do you want to go to England and how do you know that you want to become a nurse. That was my first interview ever and I guess that I was totally unprepared for most of his questions. I was very shy and the bastard turned down my request and denied me the visa. During those years the British Embassy had been giving out visas left and right to anyone who wanted to go to England. Of course we were all disappointed.

I wrote to my cousin Linda and told her that the British Embassy had denied me the visa. She said forget them, why don't you come to the United States instead. The U.S. Embassy was issuing student's visas very easily at that time also. All you needed was an acceptance letter from a college, and a place to stay and you were good to go. I received my acceptance letter from a reputable college, and a letter from one of my mother's friends stating that she would allow me to reside with her while I was in school. I took both of those letters to the American Embassy in Georgetown, and just like that I was granted a student's visa and that's how I came to the United States of America forty three years ago, and I have never once regretted that move.

Coming To America

The night before my departure to the U.S., my grandmother gave me a farewell party and invited my friends, it was bitter sweet, I was happy to leave for the opportunities the U.S. had to offer, but I was also very sad leaving all of my friends and family behind, especially my grandmother she had raised me and she had done an excellent job. To me she was my mother, she took care of me from infancy to young adulthood, and she had instilled in me certain values and etiquette which I have cherished all of my life. With her discipline and up bringing I have always managed to make the right decisions when it counted most.

It was very cold when I arrived, it was the third week of November the flight was very long and I was tired. The very next day reality started to set in. It was snowing I had never seen snow before this was simply amazing. I thought that coming from such a small village I would never survive in a place like NYC.

Linda knew her way around, and she advised us on what we should do. The day after my arrival my cousin Marissa and I went job hunting. We were given instructions on how to take the subway to get around, and where to go and look for jobs. No one came with us we were on our own. I was scared I had no clue where I was going neither did Marissa it was like the blind leading the blind. Somehow we found the employment agency and we began our job search. Many vacancies were advertised but neither one of us had a clue what we wanted to do or what we were qualified to do, since neither one of us had ever worked one day of our lives or had any type of job training. That's great no job experience and no clue what we wanted to do, we just wanted to work so that we could start living the American dream. Jobs were a dime a dozen, it was very easy to obtain jobs. There were lots of positions listed on the walls at the employment agency. A very large man came up to us and asked what type of jobs we were looking for, without hesitation Marissa shouted porter. Both the man and I started laughing she had no clue what a porter did. He asked us how old we were, I guess we looked much younger than our ages, when we told him that we were eighteen and nineteen years old, he did not believe us. He said that we looked about thirteen and fourteen years old, and that we should both be in school. He asked us to show him the back of our hands, and that was enough proof to confirm our ages.

Linda told us to take whatever jobs were available. I was hired for a job as a machine operator I never had any sewing lessons, never used a sewing machine before, but I listened to my cousin Linda and lied about having experience with machine operations. She said that the company would train us for whatever jobs we took. The job required being able to handle industrial sized sewing machines I was required to sew the edges of large bolts of canvas to keep it from unraveling. The man asked me if I knew how to use the machine I lied and said yes. He showed me how to thread it, it wasn't easy the thread had to be passed through several holes, and every time I started to sew, the thread came out of the eye of the needle, and I kept calling him to help me rethread. That was very frustrating for me and I assume for him also. I must have called that man every few minutes throughout that morning. At lunch time he came over to me and said look Miss I need someone who can handle this machine, I need someone with experience. I will pay you for the entire day, but please do not come back after lunch. When I got home, I blamed Linda for telling me that I should take whatever job came along.

A few weeks later my other cousin Dawn arrived in the States, she also stayed with us, we were looking for an apartment, all of us could no longer live with my mother's friend we were too many. My cousin Dawn and I both got jobs at the same factory we were pasting samples of fabrics onto sheets of paper to make sample booklets. The samples came through on a conveyer belt that meant that we had to work very fast. I got the hang of that job, and I was doing very well with that. I noticed that my face was always very itchy, my eyes were very red, I was always scratching my face and rubbing my eyes. Even after I got home but I had no clue what was wrong. Someone told me that a lot of the materials had fiberglass in them and that I was probably allergic to that. At times the itch was so unbearable, that I made frequent trips to the bathroom to wash my face with cold water this gave me temporary relief.

Debra was the boss's wife she was short skinny and had a very loud mouth. She had long stringy blonde hair, which was always un-kept. She wore high heels and short dresses as she walked around the factory yelling and screaming at everyone and everything all day long. She was a chain smoker. After one of my bathroom trips to wash my face, Debra was waiting outside the door for me. She asked me why I was making so many trips to the bathroom, I told her that I was allergic to some of the material which was causing me to scratch constantly, and the only relief was washing my face with cold water. She said honey you cannot leave the conveyer belt so often to wash your face you have to do that on your own time and not on the boss' time.

One day after I returned from my lunch break, the supervisor pulled me aside to a private area and told me that there were a couple of people there from the immigration department, who were asking about me and if I worked there. He told me that I should be very careful. I was so scared I was trembling. I grabbed my coat and bag and flew out of there like a bat out of hell. My heart was pounding, I could hear every beat. I kept looking behind me all the way home. I never went back to the factory I was not supposed to be working. I came to the U.S. on a student's visa I did not have permission to work and anyone found working would immediately face deportation. That's a crime and once you were sent back home, it was a very shameful situation, because the villagers laughed and made fun of your unfortunate situation. A lot of people were deported back to their countries for working illegally.

Linda once again advised me on how to handle this situation. She told me that I could no longer work in my correct name, because that's how the immigration was able to trace my activities in the first place, by my social security number. She told me that I needed to go back to the social security office and apply for a new card in a different name. She also told me to say that I was from the U.S. Virgin Islands and I wouldn't need any proof of citizenship. I did exactly what she told me to do, and a new card was issued to me I was never asked to show any proof of identity.

With my new card and fake name Patricia I began my job search. I found a job as a filing clerk with a large wholesale corporation in NYC. The home office was located on 32nd street in one of the skyscrapers. It was a beautiful building, the location was perfect, and it was a vast difference from the factory I had worked in before. I was able to sit at a desk to do my job, I did not have to stand all day the environment was much more conducive to my health and the people that worked there were in a totally different class from the factory workers. I met Ali there she and I had the same job description we were file clerks, we were about the same age, she had just graduated high school, and that was her first job. She was African American very pretty and personable, she taught me a lot about American culture especially since I was so new to the country.

She introduced me to some of the foods, and she definitely helped me with choosing my wardrobe. Every pay day we went shopping, she dressed very nicely everything was always coordinated. She helped me to choose the appropriate climate wardrobe. In Guyana there's only one climate and that's hot so all of the clothes I brought with me were summer clothes. We became best friends, she lived in the Bronx with her dad and step mother, her biological mother had died. Apparently her step mom was not very kind to her, and she wanted to leave home, but she didn't think that she would make it on her own. She had two boy-friends, one was Frank and the other was John. Both of them were very good to her. She was confused about a lot of things and couldn't make up her mind about which one she wanted to be with.

I told her about the pros and cons to make a list and see who had the most pros and probably go for that one. She did and decided that Frank was the better person she knew this all along, because he was more responsible and wanted to marry her. She also said that John was a lot more fun to be with he always took her out to discos and showed her a good time. And most importantly he was a much better lover in bed than Frank. But John was not ready to settle down. She settled for Frank he had a good job at the bank, he was college educated, he was ready to settle and he would be a good provider. Frank also loved her very much. They became engaged and she seemed to be very happy. Wedding plans were made, she asked me to be her maid of honor, and I accepted.

The wedding was beautiful the bride was gorgeous, my gown was peach colored I also looked beautiful. Her older sister was a hairstylist in Harlem, and she did our hair for the wedding. Everything seemed fine, she was happy to have her own home, then one day Ali told me that she had been seeing John again, she had been sneaking around with him. I told her that Frank would kill her if he found out and that she needed to stop that. The next day when she came to work, she told me that she couldn't sleep all night thinking about what I told her, and that she would not be seeing John anymore. She became pregnant shortly afterwards and she asked me to be the God mother of her child, and I accepted.

The company was moving their home office to Secaucus NJ, to their own building and all of the employees were offered to keep their positions if they were willing to commute to NJ. Ali did not stay with the company she had a new baby to take care of. Some of us took the challenge, but the commute was hell, there were too many exchanges to be made just to get to work.

Reunited

My mom had made the trip from England to New York exactly one year after I arrived here. That was in 1970. I had not seen my mom since 1963 when she left Guyana for England. She looked different, she looked a little frail she was thinner than I remembered. We asked her about that she said that in England people rationed their food, they were not starving, but they did not indulge in overeating. I felt very strange reuniting with her surprisingly I didn't feel the connection I had as a little girl. My mom connected with some of her friends who had migrated from Guyana to the states while she was in England. As a matter of fact, she had many friends over here she had not seen for a long time. One of them was Mr. B the station master from Beterverwagting, the one who was always nice to me. He had moved to the states with all of his children, and I had not seen them in a very long time. We visited him and his family in N.J. they lived in a very large house. He had a new wife and two little boys added to his entourage. I was very happy to connect with Kathryn again we hadn't seen each other for many years. We started visiting each other and partying every weekend.

I was still corresponding with Marty, but he seldom wrote back. I was still in love with him I wanted him to come to the states so that we could be together. All of my friends were telling me that I should forget about him and find someone here. My girlfriend Kayla introduced me to her cousin Kyle. He was short with slightly bowed legs, and very cute. We started dating, but I still couldn't get Marty out of my mind. My friends were all sexually active I couldn't believe that I was the only one who never had sex. I thought that they were all virgins. Because of my upbringing and faith at that time I insisted on abstinence. My grandmother had told me that sex is forbidden before marriage and only loose women indulged, and I believed her.

I celebrated my 21st birthday with my friends and family, it was a grand affair. Everyone looked beautiful, we all wore formal attire. The thought kept bugging me 21 years old and still a virgin, in some ways I was proud of my virginity, but I also felt that I was old enough to have the experience and be like the rest of my friends. But still in the back of my mind I wanted Marty to be the one to take my virginity because he was my first love.

Kyle and I continued dating, and eventually I gave in, I decided that I would have sex with him I wanted to experience what everyone else had experienced. One Saturday evening we went to the movies, and after the movies we both agreed to go to a hotel. This must have been the most awkward moment of my life. There was no rushing desire on my part, we both got undressed and got into the bed, then he made the move I don't think that he had a lot of experience himself, and up until that moment I did not tell him that I was a virgin. We did and it was painful in more than one ways. I was overwhelmed he seemed surprised and he said that he didn't know that I was a virgin, and that I should have told him. I couldn't wait to tell my friends that I was no longer a virgin. We left the hotel and he took me home. We became closer, and my feelings for him grew, I had fallen in love with him. He was living in N.J. at that time while I lived in Brooklyn. My job commute was horrible, I needed a different job my friend Kathryn was working as a coding clerk for a very large newspaper company in Newark N.J., and she told me that I should apply, because there were vacancies. She arranged an interview, and I got the job. That made my life so much easier the commute to Newark every day was not bad.

One year after my mom arrived in the states, her twin sister came over on a visitor's visa and they were reunited after being apart for several years. The boy Linda dated in high school back home migrated to the states, and shortly after they got married. He enlisted in the army and they moved to Louisiana. Marissa and Dawn were married shortly after, both marrying their boyfriends from back home. Marissa moved to Canada with her husband. Dawn stayed on in Brooklyn with her husband. I was the only one out of the group that had not gotten married. My original social network had broken up.

I started to notice that Kyle was telling a lot of lies, he made dates with me but he wouldn't show up and there was always some sorry excuse. My new job was located in the same city as Kyle lived in. It was actually walking distance from his apartment building. I thought that this was a good thing, we were closer and I would be able to see him a lot more. One evening I visited him and all of a sudden he started rushing me out of his apartment and told me that I had to leave. He made up some sorry excuse I can't remember what that excuse was about, but as I was leaving, I passed a young lady she was about my age walking towards his apartment. I was tempted to turn around and go back to his apartment, but I was never the confrontational type. He started stealing money from me he would just go into my handbag and steal my money. Whenever I confronted him, he always denied it.

That relationship became rocky it was on and off. One day I received a call from his cousin Kayla she told me that Kyle had gotten married. That was a shock and a huge blow to my ego I wondered where I went wrong, what the hell had happened I was truly upset. Then she told me that he didn't want me to know anything, that she should keep it a secret. On my way to work one day I was passing by his apartment building, he saw me and started calling my name, I totally ignored him and that was the last time I had heard from him or seen him.

A few years later we met at a social function and we did speak to each other. He told me that he was a professional photographer. He was looking for business he gave me his cards and asked me to tell my friends about his business. He actually did excellent work his studio was located in South Plainfield. He did some photography work for me which I was very satisfied with, but his prices were always on the higher end. A friend of my brother Adrian was getting married his name is Denny I sent him to Kyle's studio to see some of his work. He liked what he saw and he booked him to do his wedding pictures. Everything went well during the event, and Kyle gave a promissory date to deliver the pictures. The date Kyle promised to deliver the pictures, passed and he kept making excuses after excuses. My friend had already paid him all of the money up front, that's the way Kyle wanted it.

One Saturday Adrian and Denny decided to pay Kyle a surprise visit to his studio. This was almost one year after the wedding, when they asked him about the pictures and what was taking him so long, he tried to get snippy with them, so Adrian started walking back to his car he told him that he was going to get his machete. Kyle's wife happened to be in the studio at the time, and apparently she was able to quiet things down, she promised Denny that he would have their wedding album within a reasonable amount of time from that day and she apologized for her no good husband. After they left the studio I received a phone call from this irate mother fucker Kyle yelling and screaming at me and saying that I sent my brother to threaten him. I politely told him that he was a thief and that he deserved what he got, and then I slammed the phone down never to hear from him again. His wife kept her word and Denny and his wife received their wedding album as she promised.

Sponsorship

I was looking for a sponsor to obtain a permanent visa and get out of my illegal status, because since I arrived in the U.S., I had been working illegally. I never started school even though I came over on a student's visa. One day I was discussing this issue with my mom and she said to me that Mr. B (the station master) said that if I carried his last name, that he would sponsor me. I looked her straight in her eyes and said to her how the hell could I possibly have his last name when he's not my father. She just looked at me and walked away never to bring that topic up again.

Mr. B was very much pro education, all of his kids were college bound he encouraged me to go to college. I had been in the country about three years and never set foot in school. I decided to enroll in county college as a business major I decided that I didn't want to be a nurse anymore. I enrolled in my correct name, but I was still working under that fake name. Kathryn introduced me to a friend of hers named Ona, we became good friends, and the three of us hung out together all of the time. One day Ona told me that the nice guy Mr. B was my dad and that Kathryn was really my sister. I asked her what the hell she was talking about, and she told me that everyone else knew that he was my dad but that my mother didn't want to tell me the truth, since she apparently was still married to her husband when I was conceived by

Mr. B. I was shocked, embarrassed and totally pissed off but I chose not to believe what Ona had just told me. I told her that was untrue and my father was in Guyana. Everything started to fall into place, now I know why he took so much interest in me during those years in BV. I was twenty two years old when I found this out, but I still refused to believe it because I felt that if it was so my mother or Mr. B should have been the ones to tell me. I never asked either one of them if that was the truth and for that I truly regret.

After I started college, Ona introduced me to a middle aged couple who had started a transportation business, and they were looking for someone to schedule appointments and dispatch the drivers to take the residents to their appointments. Because I was in school that was the ideal job for me. I had lots of time to study while working. My grades were excellent. The job was done in an office from their home and during down time I helped to clean up. They were a very busy couple with demanding jobs. She was the director of nurses of a very large nursing home, and he was an administrator. He also was the pastor of a Baptist church.

At that time I had a very small apartment in a two family house, and my apartment was on the upper level. The man who lived below was the most miserable person on earth, every time you moved he complained. Many weekends Ona stayed with me, we kept a party one Saturday night with some of our friends we danced and had fun, after the party we cleaned up and took all of the garbage out before going to bed. Very early the next day the owner of the house showed up at my apartment with her husband, they asked to come in. She said that the tenant below had called complaining that we were partying and had been making noise all night and he couldn't sleep. She herself was in disbelief, because as she looked around everything was clean and in order, there were no signs of any partying activities from the night before. I told her that I had two friends visiting who were still there, Ona and Kayla, I said that I was sick of that man he was always complaining about everything every time you walked he complained. I told her that I would be moving soon because I couldn't stand his constant complaints anymore. After they left we laughed out loudly and celebrated more, because he looked like a damn fool, there was no evidence of any party activities. I was looking for an apartment to move into and my new boss offered me to move in with them, they had a third floor apartment. I was offered in exchange of helping around the house that was a good deal for me.

They invited me to church one Sunday and I went. I was brought up Episcopalian, but during that time I was not going to church. That was my very first exposure to the Baptist faith, the service was very different from what I was accustomed to. My eyes caught onto the organist he was about 5'11" with light complexion. He played the organ, and sang very well, I was instantly interested in getting to know him, so I started going to church regularly. Eventually I was introduced to him and we started talking and calling each other on the phone. He was very mannerly polite and attentive. When I introduced him to my family, they all liked him instantly because of his mannerism. His name is Monroe. He wore his hair in a large afro, this was the mid seventy's and the "fro" was definitely in. We were both in our twenty's I was two years older than him.

He lived at home with his mother two sisters and a couple of nieces. I found it strange that at his age twenty four years old he did not have a real job, his only income came from him playing the organ at church every Sunday and whenever there was an event going on at church. He was not in school either, so I felt that there were no excuses for him not to have a real job. I asked him what he wanted to do with his life, what he saw for himself in the future, he had no clue. I suggested that he got himself a job and he agreed with me. I also told him that since his mom was a single parent, he should give her some money each time he got paid to assist her with the bills he was too old for her to be supporting him and he agreed with me. I spoke with the Stevens those were the people I worked for and asked them to offer him a job at the nursing home. He was offered a job as an orderly during the night shift. He took the job, and that was a good start. Everything seemed to be moving in the right direction.

I was very busy with my studies, and had changed my major from business to nursing. I was accepted into the two year nursing program at the county college, the program was very demanding there was not much time for anything else but studying. Monroe visited frequently, many times I asked him not to visit since I needed to study, but he still showed up. On one occasion I got so angry with him because I was studying for a final exam and he showed up. I rudely said to him, you are interrupting my studies I do not have the time to spend with you. He apologized and said that he would just sit there and watch TV while I studied, that in itself was a distraction. Somehow I felt guilty for being so rude to him, thinking that he was so much in love with me that he was willing to sit and watch TV while I studied. He stayed for a while before leaving.

Some things were beginning to bother me about him he seemed to lack insight and ambition into his future. So one day I asked him if he had any plans in furthering his education, of course he had no plans, this never crossed his mind. I told him that if he wanted to be with me, he would have to think of something, either learn a trade, or enroll in college. I needed to be with someone who was ambitious and wanting to improve their situation. We discussed many options, and I came up with the suggestion of him enrolling in college to take classes towards a major in music. He immediately agreed to this, since he really loved music. I suggested that he could teach music after he obtained his degree, he was actually excited. Even though he was so talented in playing the organ, he did it by ear, he could not read music, but he could play just about anything that was totally amazing to me.

The decision was made, and I helped him with the application process so that he could start county college. He enrolled and started taking classes. By now we had been dating for one and a half years, and decided that we should get married. I had two semesters left to graduate nursing school, I also was feeling good about Monroe being enrolled in college, he was finally working towards a better future, and we would both have professional jobs doing what we both liked.

I Do

On January 10th 1978 we said I do's, we were married by the pastor I wore a white two piece suit, and he wore an off white suit. We had just the immediate families, his and mine and dinner. There was no honeymoon since I was still in school. It was in the middle of winter, and one of the worst winters I have so far experienced. It was one of the stormiest winters it snowed heavily for days on end. Many days everything was shut down. The trains, buses all public transportation came to a stand-still. The snow was so high that nothing could get through. Every morning the phone rang, it was the college calling to say that classes were once again cancelled, I was always happy because it gave me more time to do my studies towards my final exams, I aced all of my exams that semester.

I was so busy with school and being married, looking forward to graduation and studying for my nursing boards that I did not realize that I had missed a period. I said no way I could not be pregnant even though I was not taking any precautions against getting pregnant. A few weeks later I went to the Dr. to confirm what I already knew, I was indeed pregnant.

Graduation was in May, and I was four months pregnant. I was very happy to be done with school. I started working at the same nursing home as a graduate nurse, that Monroe worked at we worked different shifts. I chose to work at the nursing home, even though it wasn't my ideal choice, but I felt that it would be good for me until after I had the baby, then I'd apply to a hospital after I returned to work from my maternity leave. I was just happy to finally be making a decent salary.

We had our first apartment together, and everything was going well, the only furniture we had was our bedroom furniture. We hung sheets for window coverings, and in the living room there was a single four tier bookcase where I kept all of my books, since I still had to study for my upcoming board's exam. Monroe worked the day shift and went to school in the evenings, I worked the evening shift. I started to realize that Monroe was hanging out with some less than desirable company. I asked him why he was being so friendly with those low life's he always had a lame excuse, such as I'm a friendly guy and I like talking to people. I also started noticing that he was extremely jealous of my relationship with my family and friends.

I was at home studying and the doorbell rang, when I answered it, there was a woman standing at the door, she looked familiar and that's because she was always roaming around the hallways of the apartment complex, and she always appeared to be high as a kite. I was stunned that she was at my door I asked her how may I help you her response was I'm here to see that brother that lives here, I told her that she had the wrong apartment. She said no I'm at the right apartment and I'm here to see that light skinned brother I think that his name is Monroe. I was stunned, I couldn't believe my ears, I asked her what the hell she wanted with him, and she said that she wanted to tell him something. I told her to get the hell away from my door and that she should never come here again. She was so high she couldn't even hold her head up for one moment. She looked into my apartment and when she saw the bookcase full of books, she apparently was amazed. She said oh my God what are you doing with all of those books, are you a doctor or something.

I slammed the door shut and she left. When Monroe came home I asked him how he became friends with this woman that she came to see him, of course he said that he is a friendly person and he speaks to everyone and I said even the damn junkies you are inviting them to our apartment. I quoted one of my grandmother's favorite sayings, "show me your company and I'll tell you who you are."

Now I'm beginning to realize that I don't really know the man to whom I'm married. Even though we dated for one and a half years before we got married, I never really had much time to hang out with him and meet his friends, since I was always studying, and he frequently told me that he didn't have many friends. One day I came home and one of his guy friends was visiting whom he had mentioned a few times before, but I had never met him. To my surprise, his friend had the appearance of a homosexual person. His pants and shirt were tighter than I would have ever dreamed of wearing mine. His hair was spiked and colored red and his mannerism was definitely "girlish."

It's not my intention to offend anyone, but I never imagined that my husband's very "good" friend was a homosexual. I was speechless at first I wasn't sure how to handle the situation, then I thought that I should at least be polite. Monroe introduced his friend to me and as soon as he did, all hell broke loose. I asked him if he was the very "good" friend that he always spoke about and he said that he was. I said I can't believe what I'm seeing here your friend is obviously gay, and I would like to know what the hell the two of you are doing in here. I told his friend to get the hell out of my apartment, but he just sat there in disbelief, he didn't move he just sat there looking at me. I repeated myself very slowly I said I would like you to get up right now and leave this apartment and you are never welcomed here again. He got up and left very quietly.

Monroe was so angry with me that he went into a wild rage I had never in my entire life seen anything like that before. He cursed me out calling me the biggest fucking bitch and every other degrading word one can think of. He then went over to the book shelf, grabbed each and every book off the shelves and threw them against the walls in a mad rage. I stood there in the middle of the living room just looking at him I couldn't believe what I was seeing. I cursed him back and I told him that all the people he hung out with seemed to be some sort of degenerate. I told him that his friend was not allowed to come back to our apartment. I was just beginning to see the light. I was planning on leaving Monroe, and discussed this with my friend Remy, she told me that I should not leave until I filed and obtained my green card. She said after all you've gone through with this fool you should at least get something out of it. She introduced me to an attorney who filed my papers for permanent residency. I was now on my way to freedom from my illegal status.

He left home a little late one day, he was running to catch the bus to go to school he was wearing platform shoes, and twisted his ankle, and ended up fracturing his leg. When he came home, he had a full length cast on his right leg and crutches he was not allowed to do any weight bearing on that leg. We didn't have a car as yet so we took the bus or train everywhere we went. Here we go again, I'm expecting in a few months, I'm working and soon to be on maternity leave and my husband is presently disabled. It was mid semester and I suggested that we call his instructors and ask them to mail his assignments so that he could complete the semester and not lose any credits. He agreed and I started making phone calls to his instructors telling them his sad story and asking them to send the necessary material so he can complete his studies for that period.

All but one of them agreed to send the assignments. I asked her why would she not send the assignments, even after I told her the reason, and she said that it's mid semester and he only showed up in her class once, she felt that it would be a waste of her time. I was truly embarrassed and thanked her for her time. I confronted Monroe with this because he left every day to go to school he lied and said that whenever he got to her classroom, her classes were always cancelled. I said to him that never happens there will always be a replacement or an alternative. I said I'm done with this bull shit, I'm not your mother, and I'm not going to keep pushing you to get an education to better your position in life. That's all Monroe needed to hear, he also was done with college. I realized that he didn't like to work, he had poor work ethics he called out sick frequently and he lacked ambition. We were total opposites, but not compatible ones.

Every time we visited his mother she told him no matter what arguments you and your wife may have, you should never hit a pregnant woman. I never really understood why she kept telling him that, because he had never hit me or attempted to do so. I just couldn't understand why she felt that it was important for him to hear this every time we visited.

During all of this time I was studying at home for my nursing Boards, I had to remain focused. The exam was in July and I had to wait for several weeks before the results came back. That was a nerve wrecking wait, I worried a whole lot. Finally the results arrived in the mail in the brown manila envelope, that's all I needed to see, because we all knew that a brown manila envelope from the State Board of Nursing meant that you passed your exam, and anyone receiving a white envelope unfortunately did not pass. I was so happy I started jumping up and down, totally excited, actually I was elated. Monroe had brought the mail in, he stood there looking at me going crazy and he told me to stop jumping since I was pregnant. I stopped jumping up and down, and decided to open the mail, but at the same time started to panic, what if I didn't pass, I would have celebrated in vain. The results were good I was now a Registered Nurse. I must have called everyone I knew with the news. The best part of that was the increase in my salary from graduate nurse to registered nurse.

Labor Pains

Our baby was born in the fall, she was delivered by C-section. She was the most beautiful baby I have ever laid eyes on. I woke up around three in the morning to this terrible pain, it was a Sunday morning it scared me, but the pains were coming far apart. I went back to bed, but I couldn't fall asleep because I was very worried about the contractions. I am a chicken when it comes to pain, my tolerance is very low. Every time I had a contraction I got onto my knees. My Doctor had told me to wait until my contractions were three minutes apart before going to the hospital at least I think that's what he said. I waited until they were three minutes apart the hospital was not very far away, so we called our friends Remy and Will to take me to the hospital as planned. We didn't have a car of our own. I think that Will ran every red light on the way to the hospital, wanting to get there fast.

Upon my arrival I was wheeled to the maternity ward, soon after I was examined and the nurse told me that I was 2 cm dilated, this was at twelve noon on Sunday. The contractions kept coming my lower back felt as though it was about to explode. I had been planning on having natural child birth delivery. I had taken Lamaze classes, how brave of me. This choice of delivery should only be attempted by brave people not cowards like me. The contractions were coming so fast that I hardly had time to catch my breath in between contractions. I was begging for pain meds, but I was denied each time. I was given a mask to breathe in and out of, this was supposed to relax me and take my mind off the pain, believe me it didn't work. The nurse assigned to me was a middle aged woman. I found her to be very rude and lacking empathy, when I asked her to please hold my hand because I was so scared, she refused she told me that I should hold on to the bed rail, and she left the room. I was so miserable I couldn't find a comfortable position for one second. Sometimes I screamed from pain or from fear. There was no progress I had been there for hours and I was still 2 cm dilated, the contractions were relentless they decided to start an intravenous with a Pitocin drip, to increase my contractions, and hooked me up to a fetal monitor.

This just made things worse for me I kept feeling as though I had to go to the bathroom I kept calling the nurse frequently, I wasn't allowed to get out of bed they kept offering me the bed pan, and each time it was a false alarm. I believe that I had taken leave of my senses, I was over the top. That mean old nurse came into my room and said I can't believe it I just found out that you are a Registered Nurse and you are behaving this way. I said to her you mean old bitch what does that have to do with anything I am human first I have feelings just like anyone else am I supposed to suppress my feelings just because I'm a nurse. I said I bet you don't have any kids of your own you have never gone through labor and delivery, just get out of my room and don't come back in here I would like to have a different nurse. After she left my room, I heard the nurses talking and laughing loudly at the nurses' station. This made me so mad the nerve of them to be having fun while I was suffering. So I got onto my knees in the middle of the bed, I held onto both bed rails and started shaking the hell out of those rails. Intravenous tubing, fetal monitors everything became tangled up. Within a few seconds the entire staff came running into my room, they couldn't believe what they were seeing. They tried prying my hands off the rail, I had such a grip on those rails, they had a hard time getting my hands off, and then they had to untangle all of the I.V tubing and wires from the fetal monitor. I said to them how dare all of you to sit out there talking and laughing out loudly while I'm in here suffering.

Another contraction started, and I asked Monroe to hold the mask to my face so that I could breathe in and out of it. He did and at the same time old nurse Ratched came into the room, she took the mask from him and gave it to me and said that he couldn't hold it I had to be the one to hold it myself. I said what difference does it make who holds the mask I took the mask from him and threw it as hard as I could against the wall, and told her that she should take that fucking mask and shove it up her ass. That nurse got on her hands and knees and crawled out of my room, she never came back in. Monroe was laughing, he said that I shouldn't have done that, so I asked him to leave my room also and he did. It was so funny watching her crawl out of my room, but at that time I couldn't laugh the pain was unbearable. Now I really had to go to the bath room I dare not bother those nurses again after all that commotion I had just created. So I just pissed in the bed, I didn't care. Looking back, I really thought I had taken leave of my senses. I was really exhausted it was a very long day, the contractions were still coming very close, and every time they examined me, I was still the same 2cm dilated no progress from that end.

Finally my room became a very busy spot everyone was in there the fetal monitor was showing some sorts of fetal distress this meant emergency C-section. Nurse Ratched all of a sudden was very nice she showed empathy and started to explain to me exactly what was going to happen now. She told me that I was going to be prepped for the surgery and explained everything she was going to do, also the fact that a Foley catheter had to be inserted. I tried protesting to that, but I knew that was a losing battle. She even told me that my doctor made me wait too long, that he should have taken me to surgery a long time ago. Everything was done very fast, and I was rushed to the OR. The contractions were intense, my lower back felt as though it was about to explode. The entire surgical team was waiting in the operating room when I arrived everyone was all ready to go. I had another contraction I tried to get out of the stretcher, but I was strapped in I couldn't get up. I asked the anesthesiologist who was standing next to me to please give me something for the pain he said he couldn't give me any sedation until they were actually ready to start surgery. Each time a contraction came I grabbed his hands and put it to my lower back for support he was very kind and went along with my madness.

I looked up between contractions and saw my doctor standing there. He was an older doctor and very distinguished. I told him to please hurry up and do the surgery I want this to be over with. He smiled and said to me that he was waiting for his assistant, I asked him where his assistant was and he told me that he had just called him at home and his wife told him that he was out for a joy ride and he should be back soon. I went off on that doctor, I told him that he didn't need to wait for some stupid assistant, that he was doing this for many years he had lots of experience and he had my permission to go ahead and do the surgery all by himself. After my outburst I looked up and everyone was standing there just looking at me over their masks. Again I had made a complete ass of myself and I was totally embarrassed.

That's the last thing I remembered, until they woke me up and told me that I had a beautiful baby girl who weighed in at seven pounds and twelve ounces at nine thirty p.m. The nurse came into my room with a syringe in her hand, I asked her what that was and she said that she was going to give me a shot of Demerol I told her that I didn't need it I didn't have any pain, but she insisted I take it, so I did.

The next morning the day shift nurses were all talking to me and addressing me by my name, so I asked one of them how she knew me, she said from last night, and she smiled. I apologized to her and asked her to please tell everyone that I was truly sorry for my behavior. Once I saw my beautiful baby girl, I realized that every bit of that labor pain was well worth it. My recovery was uneventful and we were home in three to four days. I was so proud and happy when I left the hospital with my precious little bundle of joy all wrapped up in her little white furry winter outfit. We named her Rebecca. This was a happy and joyous time for both of us. Friends and family were visiting everyone wanted to meet our little bundle of joy. We had a one bed room apartment Rebecca's bassinet and crib were set up in the bed room with her bassinet right next to my side of the bed.

Monroe's True Colors

This happiness did not last very long, soon after Rebecca was born things started to change. Monroe's true colors were about to come out. I was home on maternity leave, and he was still in the cast and crutches, so he too was on disability, what a way to start a family. Whenever Rebecca cried, he'd say don't pick her up unless it's time to feed her, or if she's wet, because if you do she'll be spoilt. I said to him that's the most ridiculous thing I have ever heard, and whenever my baby cries, I will pick her up soothe her and comfort her. He claimed that was the way his mother raised them. I reminded him that I was not his mother and I would do it my way. I was getting to know him a lot better now and I did not like the things that I was seeing. Most of it was actually frightening. There were lots of issues on morality that were beginning to really bug me. While we argued over this issue, he pulled out a joint from nowhere and started smoking it right in the bedroom with our newborn baby. I asked him to stop that, I said that's not good for me and especially not for Rebecca, he came right over to me, took a long drag on the joint and blew it out right into my face as he laughed and walked away. Of course this started another argument, I called him a no good son of a bitch, and I told him that I would take Rebecca and leave. He came over to me and slapped me so hard in my face, that everything turned black. I believe I was out for a few seconds or so. After realizing what had happened, I called my mother to come over and she did. She talked to him and told him never to do that again, she also told him that if any man had ever hit her, that she would fight him back she would not take that from any one.

If I had any sense, I would have left that mother fucker right then and there, but I didn't. I thought that we could work things out nonviolently, but that was just the beginning of many fights to come. We fought over everything, I realized that I didn't even know whom I had married, he was totally different from that loving, caring and soft spoken person I had met and fallen in love with. Our marriage had just begun, and it already was on the rocks. I wanted to do everything in my ability to save our marriage, even though I knew that the odds were stacking up. The main reason I wanted to work at saving our marriage, was because of the fact that I did not grow up with either one of my parents, and I was determined that my child would have both of her parents.

I began detecting signs of extreme jealousy in Monroe, whenever I spoke with my friends on the phone male or female it created problems. He accused me of having an affair with my best friend's husband. He claimed Rebecca could be Will's child because both he and Will were of light complexion, so he could not be certain Rebecca was his child. This was the most outrageous accusation I had heard from him so far, and it hurt me very much. Immediately I called my girlfriend Remy who is Will's wife and related to her what Monroe had just accused me of. She came right over to our apartment she had a few words to say to Monroe. She told him he ought to be ashamed of himself, and maybe he is projecting his behavior and life style onto me, but in our circle we do not operate in this manner. He complained about the way I dressed, about my make-up, my hair about everything I did. Each and every time I left the apartment to go out, he accused me of going to meet with another man. He was beginning to wear me down. I tried to change my style of dress and not wear make-up just to keep the peace, but he still found something to complain about. Whenever I visited my mom she asked how I was doing, she was very observant and had noticed I was not looking my best. She knew I always dressed nicely, and all of a sudden my appearance had taken a dive. I reassured her everything was fine, but having a new baby kept me very busy with not much time left for myself.

We were invited to a house party at Mr. B's home, and all of my friends were there. Everyone was having a good time but me. I was not dancing or having fun because I knew Monroe would be pissed off, and when we got home he would accuse me of having had another man there. Kathryn asked me if I wasn't feeling well, I said I'm fine and asked her why. She told me I didn't seem to be happy and wondered if something was bothering me. She knew I loved to party and couldn't understand why I wasn't dancing and having fun like everyone else. She knew me better than anyone else and before I met him, Kathryn Ona and I were party animals. We partied every weekend, we loved dancing, we were a happy and care free group of friends who were always the life of the party. I didn't tell her the real reason I wasn't dancing and having a good time, because I was too ashamed to let her know what I was experiencing with Monroe, I wanted to keep it a secret and try to work things out with him.

Upon completion of my grocery shopping, I called Monroe on the pay phone and asked him to call the cab company and have them dispatch a cab to my location since I did not have their phone number to call them myself. As soon as I hung up the phone, I saw a yellow cab which I flagged down I was anxious to get home to Rebecca. When I arrived home he asked if the cab came to pick me up. I told him after I got off the phone I saw a yellow cab, and flagged it down. To my surprise I had made a bad decision. He became so angry, he started cursing and calling me names. He said the cab driver was my man, I had made a fool of him and he would never be able to use that cab company again. He was so angry, he took the cartoon of eggs I had just bought and smashed it on the floor. I told him I had enough of his irrational behavior, and I was leaving. I took Rebecca, and as I was heading for the door, he grabbed her from me and left the apartment. On his way out he said I would never get her back. I was scared, I didn't want him causing her any harm, he was an idiot and I thought he might do something stupid just to get back at me. I called Remy and told her what had just taken place. She and Will came right over and drove me to Monroe's mother's place. When we arrived his mother said he did go there with Rebecca, but he had left. I was very nervous and not sure what to do next. Remy and Will suggested I should go to the precinct and make a complaint. We did, I was made aware he had just as much rights to Rebecca as I did and the only thing I could do, would be to take him to court and fight for custody rights. I was devastated I didn't know what to do, I was afraid for my baby's safety and all I wanted was to have Rebecca back. Then Monroe called and said the only way you will be able to get Rebecca back is if you come back home. I went back home for Rebecca's sake, I couldn't bear to be away from my baby not even for one day. She was only a few months old and I was concerned for her well-being.

The abuse continued, it was mostly psychological, but at times there was pushing and shoving, he was always trying to belittle me and accuse me of things I had no interest in. At five feet three inches tall and weighing one hundred and twenty pounds he insisted I was too fat, this was shortly after Rebecca's birth and I had already lost all of the weight I had gained during my pregnancy.

I left with my baby on a few other occasions, and each time he came crying and begging me to come back. He claimed he missed and loved both Rebecca and I and he would do whatever it took to make things better between us. He claimed he had learned his lesson and promised he would never hit me again. He asked the pastor to speak with me about taking him back and foolishly I went back with him. Each time I went back with Monroe he started his crap immediately, mainly accusing me of having other men with him and making threats to me.

Once I even went to a shelter for battered women, I didn't have to go there, but I was tired of involving my family into this mess I had gotten myself into, and actually I was ashamed of my situation, I wanted everyone to believe everything was just fine. The shelter was very clean and accommodating, and the woman in charge told me I didn't fit the profile. I asked her what she meant, and she explained by saying the majority of women who seek shelter there were usually very badly banged up and disheveled. She commented on the fact that both Rebecca and I were clean and neatly dressed and I had no visible bruises. My response to her was I may not fit the profile, but I definitely was in an ongoing abusive relationship both mental and physical and I just needed some time to sort things out without involving my family.

After a few hours, I called my cousin Dari and asked her if Rebecca and I could stay with her for the night. We stayed with her for a few days while I made other arrangements with a girlfriend of nine, her name is Jessica she was a single parent of a one year old daughter. She lived in a very large town house with a full finished one bedroom basement apartment, which Rebecca and I occupied. I was very lucky to obtain a job at a nursing home just across the street from where we were staying, this was a blessing I didn't have a car, neither did I have the means to purchase one any time soon. Jessica took Rebecca to the baby sitter with her daughter Jordan every day that was another blessing, I was surrounded by people who loved and were willing to help me through my situation. I forwarded my change of address at the post office, apparently one of Monroe's friends worked there and he gave him my new address. Monroe showed up at my door begging me to go back with him. I refused and asked him not to come back here. Surprisingly he left without incident.

Jessica had a very good job, she has an MBA and she worked for a large insurance company. One day she came home with the worst news I wanted to hear, she was being transferred out of state. I felt as though my world was crushing in on me. She saw the look on my face, and she told me that I could keep the apartment if I wanted to. That was good but I didn't know how I would get my baby to the sitter since I didn't have a car, and there was no one close to me that I knew, this was a disaster. I called my mother and told her my problem, I asked her if she would come and live with us, so that she can help me out with the baby sitting issue. I knew that she was in between jobs, and this could have been possible. She refused, she told me that she had already promised someone to work for them and she couldn't take it back. I told her that I was sure that person would understand and not hold that against her. She refused she did not even give it a second thought. I was so upset with my mom and couldn't understand how she would not want to help me, but remember she didn't raise me, so obviously that motherly instinct was not present. I said thank you very much, and I did not speak to my mom for several months after that.

I couldn't keep the apartment or the job I needed to be more centrally located, where I would have easier access to public transportation. I decided that I would have to give up the job and the apartment. With all of my problems, I didn't know what to do I knew that I needed to work so that I can support myself and child, and for some crazy reason, I found myself back with Monroe. This time the three of us were staying in a bedroom in his mother's house. My reason for going back with him was simply because I needed a baby sitter and I didn't have anyone else to turn to.

I started my job search, I wanted to work in a hospital, a friend of mine told me about a small community hospital in a quaint little town, she said that her niece was a nurse there and she liked it very much. I applied there for a job, and was offered the evening shift I took it. A few weeks before I started, I received a call from one of the nursing supervisors who told me that the evening shift was not available, but there was an opening on the midnight shift. Hesitantly I accepted, even though I knew that I hated that shift I had already given in my resignation from the current job.

The hospital was not close to our new place of residence, I took a bus to the train then when I got off the train I took a cab to work. I did the reverse to get back home. I hardly got any sleep, Rebecca was up, she had slept all night and she was always wide awake by the time I got home. She wanted to play, so I stayed up with her napping whenever she did, until Monroe or his mother came home which was around five o'clock in the afternoon. Then I'd try to get a few hours of sleep before getting ready for work at eleven o'clock.

One day Monroe lost it, I don't remember what happened, but he went off, he started screaming, yelling, and terrorizing every one that was in the house. He was throwing things against the wall and breaking things up, he looked like a lunatic I was afraid of him I tried to calm him down, but nothing was working. His mom called his sister Elle she lived up the street from them, she came over with her teenage son and daughter Gene and Nina. Nina had a baseball bat with her. She threatened her uncle Monroe that if he didn't stop, that she would bash his head in with the bat. Gene ran up the stairs towards his uncle and told him that if he didn't stop that both he and Nina would beat him up. He left the house after Gene approached him. I was crying everyone was crying, my poor baby was in the midst of all this, she was just a little over one year old. Elle offered me and Rebecca to stay with her until I found an apartment, she knew that I was apartment hunting I was looking for an apartment closer to my job. I accepted her offer, and Rebecca and I moved in with Elle and her three teenage kids. They were very good to us my life was in shambles, but I kept holding it together as best as I could have.

There we had peace and quiet he was not allowed to go there. Elle is one of the nicest persons I have ever met, and we have remained friends until now. Elle had a round king sized bed, with a red velvet bedspread on it and her Rebecca and I slept in that bed, with Rebecca in the middle, I can never forget that. She also babysat Rebecca at nights while I worked. I will forever be grateful to Elle.

Shortly after I found an apartment, which was located about five minutes from my new job, I was elated. It was the top floor of a two family house. It was a very old house but it was full of charm, and the location was perfect. It was a few minutes to the train station, and very close to the down town area. I couldn't have gotten anything better than that. My only problem now was getting a baby sitter. Here we go again, in a new town I'm close to my job, but I have no friends or family members close by. Once again, I allowed Monroe to come back into our lives hoping that he would change, and he promised that he would. I did need help with Rebecca.

Latoya the oldest daughter of his favorite sister was having some issues in school and she was thrown out, for some reason no other school in that district would accept her. It was almost the end of the school year, and we decided that we would take her in with us, and try to get her into the school in our town in the new school year. She was about fourteen years old at that time, and I thought that she was a nice kid. She did babysit for us and she always did an excellent job. She liked taking care of Rebecca she braided her hair and kept her very tidy. I was very happy to have her with us, and looking forward to her moving in permanently.

She went home every weekend. One day we were preparing to go out, and I couldn't find the outfit I planned on wearing. I kept my clothes in Rebecca's closet, because the apartment we lived in was very old and the closets were very small, that's the way they were made during that era. I asked Monroe if he had hidden my pants, because he always complained about my pants being too tight. He started laughing and said as much as I would love it, I wouldn't do that. He helped me to look for my pants, but we never found it. I decided to wear something else and that too was missing. I was completely baffled I didn't want to believe that Monroe was hiding my clothes.

I was talking to one of Monroe's niece's her name is Melba she had also baby sat for Rebecca during the summer. I was very fond of her, she was a good kid. I just happened to mention to her that I was missing some of my clothes, and right away she started describing them to me. She told me that Latoya her cousin had given her some clothes, and told her that someone had given the clothes to her, but since they were too small for her Latoya, she was giving them to her cousin Melba. Latoya was a big girl, I never thought that she would take my clothes she was the last person I would be suspicious of. She was much larger than me in size that I did not expect. Melba said aunty I am so sorry but I will return all of your clothes to you. I told Monroe what Melba told me about the clothes. He said I told you I didn't hide your clothes, but Latoya would have to deal with me when she comes here. Latoya had easy access to my clothes, because they were kept in Rebecca's closet and she had been sharing Rebecca's room. When Latoya returned from her weekend visit with her mom and sister, I asked her why she took my clothes and gave them away to her cousins. She tried to deny, but I told her to stop lying because I had already had proof of what she had done.

Monroe came in and went after her he called her a thief and a liar. That was not enough he started hitting her very hard all over her body I tried to get in-between the two of them, she was crying and screaming, I was yelling at him to stop hitting her he pushed me away and kept beating her. She was crying and I was crying I threatened to call the cops if he didn't stop, and that's when he stopped and walked out of the apartment. I felt so bad and wished that I had not said anything to him about the missing clothes, but I had no clue that Latoya was the culprit. My landlord complained about the noise, and they told me that they heard everything that went on upstairs. I apologized and promised that it wouldn't happen again. Latoya was very fair skinned, and she had bruises all over her body, I applied ice packs and comforted her. I apologized to her for telling him about the missing clothes. Looking back now he could have been charged for child abuse.

The weekend came around again, he took Latoya home as usual, but she never returned. Can't blame her, I would have done the same. His entire family knew what happened, and how he had beaten up Latoya. I spoke with Melba about the incident, and told her that I felt guilty because I had told him about Latoya taking my clothes. She said you shouldn't feel guilty because you had no idea that he would beat Latoya for taking your clothes. I still feel sad whenever I think about that incident.

Monroe liked driving he said he wanted to take the test to become a bus driver. I asked him if he was serious, he said yes so I gave him the money to take the test. He took the test and passed it that was very good we were both very happy. He started applying for bus driving jobs. One day we saw an ad in the newspaper for the NJ transit needing bus drivers. That would be the ideal job, the salary was excellent, plus the benefits were great. He applied for the position, and he got the job. Monroe was always lucky to get jobs he was very good looking, soft spoken and respectful. He presented himself very well. Initially people always seemed to take a likeness to him. I just hoped and prayed that Monroe would keep this job. This however was a good job, the pay was excellent, and the benefits were good. I thought that financially we should do very well. When Monroe received his first check, I told him that he should sign it over to me, he asked why. I said you haven't worked in a long time and I have been paying all of the bills by myself. He said no way, I haven't worked in a while and I need a new suit and a new pair of shoes, and I have other things to do.

We went to the grocery store, I took a cart, and Monroe took one, I wondered why we had two carts, but I thought that maybe he wanted to do a large grocery shopping. I did notice that he was only putting items into the cart that he liked. When we got up to the register, he went ahead of me and paid for his items only. I couldn't believe my eyes. I didn't say anything to him we went home and unpacked the groceries. We took taxi cabs around town all the time, because we did not have a car. I decided that it was time for us to buy a car it would make things a whole lot easier for us to get around town. I still hadn't learned to drive, that was something I had planned on obtaining soon. My first car was a used Chevy Malibu, Monroe drove the car, and I started taking driving lessons. I obtained my driving license shortly after.

We shared the car, but most of the times he had possession of the car. He took me to work every day, but most times I had to take a taxi home because he just wouldn't show up to pick me up after work. By this time I was working the second shift, three to eleven p.m.

On his days off he disappeared, he'd be gone, sometimes for two days straight without any phone calls or anything I'd have no clue where he was. Once I asked him where he was and why he didn't call he said that he was playing pool at his friend's house, and that his friend did not have a phone, so that was why I didn't hear from him. I said ok Monroe if that's the way you want it, then that's the way it will be. When I'm off and I go out and don't return or make a phone call to let you know where I am please don't be surprised, because I'll be at my friend's house playing pool also and there's no phone at that house either.

Rebecca had a very high fever and I took her to the pediatrician I took a cab, then I walked across a very busy street to get to the pharmacy to get her medication then we took a cab back home. When Monroe came home two days later, he said hello and I said hello he asked about Rebecca, I told him that she had been ill and I took her to the doctor. He went into her room to see how she was doing then he came back into the kitchen to me. He said I'm not even going to tell you where I was, because if I do you won't believe me anyway. I asked him if he hadn't noticed that I didn't ask him anything about where he was. I told him that I didn't care. He said ok, I bet that you had your man in here fucking you while I was gone. I said not only one man but I had all of the men in the entire town fucking me while you were gone for two days. This started another screaming match. My landlord was already beginning to complain about our frequent fights, and threatening to evict us if it didn't stop. Each and every time he did something wrong, he tried to make it seem as though I was the guilty party. He always projected his wrong doings onto me.

I was beginning to make friends at work, and getting to know my way around the town. I knew that I had to do something drastic I had to get him out of my life for good. He worked the evening shift and his last passenger route ended about one-thirty am, that was the time he returned the bus into the bus depot. From the depot to our apartment it took about fifteen minutes. Every day he came home at six a.m. the next morning. At first I argued with him, but then I stopped because I knew that it would soon be over. Also I tried to keep the peace, because I did not want to be given an eviction notice to leave the apartment because of constant noise and fighting. Rebecca and I had already moved too many times I needed to be the one to create some stability in our lives.

Monroe was beginning to have issues with his transit job. He had three minor accidents within a very short period of time. He was asked not to return to work after the third accident until a thorough investigation was completed. One day we were on our way out when the doorbell rang. I answered the door and the gentleman introduced himself to me. He said that he was an insurance investigator for the NJ transit, and he was here to speak with Monroe. I invited him in and brought him upstairs to the apartment. He and Monroe sat in the living-room talking about the accidents. I was lying across the bed, our bedroom and living rooms were separated by a sheer set of curtains.

I heard everything that was being said. He asked Monroe to explain exactly to him about each accident, specifically the last one. He also told him that he noticed that he was able to obtain signatures from his passengers as witnesses to all of the accidents. Monroe agreed to this. Then the investigator told him I've also noticed that this passenger signed for all three accidents, she had been on the bus each time, and he asked him if she was a regular passenger. Monroe agreed that she was. The investigator said to him, that the place where the last accident occurred that all passengers should have been off of the bus. He asked him why that passenger was still on the bus when he was heading back to the depot to drop off the bus. Monroe said oh that's some Reverend's wife and she was stranded, so I was taking the bus back to the depot, to complete my shift, then get to my car to give her a ride home.

The investigator reminded him that no passengers should have been on that bus after the last drop off point he thanked him for his cooperation, and told him that he would turn in his report to the appropriate department, and that he would be hearing from them after the investigation was completed.

After the investigator left, Monroe said to me I know that you overheard everything the investigator said but please don't let that affect you in any way. I was only trying to help out the pastor's wife by giving her a ride home. I remained very calm, but I knew at that moment why Monroe had not been coming home until six a.m. every morning, when his shift ended at one thirty a.m. He was too busy helping out the pastor's wife!

Three weeks later he received a certified letter from the N.J. department of transportation. The investigation had been completed, and they had sent him their decision. Not surprisingly, he was rightfully dismissed from the job. Once again he was out of a job.

Monroe's grandfather passed away, he had lived in Connecticut, and we were all preparing to go there for the funeral services. We had planned to leave early that morning on the day of the service because the drive to Connecticut was about three hours away. The day before we left, his sister Lindsey called he always said that she was his favorite sister. They talked on the phone, and I heard him saying oh yea that sounds like a great idea, I'll tell Adrianna that she and Rebecca can prepare to leave today with some other family member whom I didn't even know.

When he hung up the phone, he told me that he and his sister had decided that I should leave with Rebecca the night before to go to Connecticut so that he can accommodate his sister and her two kids in the car that I had bought. I said no way am I doing that, tell your sister that she and her kids should go with whomever she wishes, but she is not going to dictate my life. I also reminded him that the car was mine I'm the one who had paid for it, not him or his favorite sister Lindsey. I guess this upset him he took the phone off the hook and hit me in my face, then called me a bitch. My right eye was swollen, and black and blue. I kept applying ice packs to it I wanted the swelling to go down, because I didn't want anyone to see that I had a black eye.

The next day I covered up the bruised area with a lot of makeup and we left for Connecticut as planned to attend the funeral services. I met a lot of his family members, for the first time, I don't think anyone noticed my black eye, if they did no one asked any questions about it.

Monroe has lost his job and he's at home the accusations have now started again. Every day it's something or the other, he was always finding something to argue about there was never any peace in our home. I was going through some sort of depression at that time, but I tried to hide it I had to remain strong for Rebecca's sake. I still was not speaking to my mom for not being there for us when we needed her most. I always felt very sad and scared and often wished Monroe would die just so I could have some peace in my life. Each time I entertained those evil thoughts, I prayed to God for forgiveness. I had stopped communicating with my few good friends, because every time I got on the phone he accused me of talking about him. I had made the decision to let go of my friendships rather than have fights with him all of the time. I even tried changing my ways and beliefs, I stopped arguing back with him I stopped wearing makeup because every-time I did he accused me of going to meet my man I tried to please him, I still wanted our marriage to work.

One day I was watching TV and I saw an ad about abusive husbands. They offered a phone number to call for help which I noted. When he came home I told him about the ad, and I gave him the phone number. I asked him to please call the number, because I felt that he needed help. I also told him that I would be willing to work this through with him. He took the paper from me that I had written the phone number on, and tore it up in front of my face then he told me that he didn't need help, that I was the sick one in the relationship, therefore I should be the one to seek help. It made me aware then that Monroe enjoyed what he did he had no intentions of changing any of his behaviors, and I was the one who had to make a change.

During one of our frequent arguments I went into the bathroom to get away from him. He followed me in there and locked the door. He stood in front of the door so I couldn't get out. He accused me of having affairs with other men, and he threatened to hurt me. He terrorized me in that bathroom for about half an hour. I was crying and begging him to please let me go, Rebecca was left alone, and I just wanted to comfort her, because I knew that she was afraid. He threatened to kill me. I believed that he would, he seemed to be out of control and out of his mind. I was so afraid especially for Rebecca she was always in the midst of all this commotion, and if by chance he killed me what would happen to her who would take care of her. Eventually he opened the bathroom door and let me out. I ran to Rebecca and picked her up I did not want her to see me crying, so I tried to hold it together.

City Hall

The following day I was off from work, and as soon as Monroe left I took the opportunity to go to city hall to file a complaint against him and the threats he had made to me the day before. City hall was within walking distance from my apartment, and when I returned home Monroe was there. He asked where I was, I told him some things are better left unsaid, and it would be wise not to pursue this matter. He insisted on knowing where I was, and instead of me telling him a lie I told him I went to city hall and filed a complaint against him for the threats he made to me the day before. He had threatened to kill me, so I told him if I was ever found dead, the city would save time and money by going after him right away. There would be no need to waste the tax payer's money by conducting an intense investigation he would be the number one suspect. I guess he didn't appreciate my comments.

He grabbed me by my neck then he grabbed the butcher's knife and held it to my throat. He said I should just go ahead and kill you now. I looked around for Rebecca and she was just standing there backed up into a corner, with both of her little arms drawn backwards and her eyes were about to bulge out of their sockets. She was not quiet three years old as yet, but the fear on her face was unbearable. This was my turning point I knew I had to leave him for good. I couldn't bear to see my little girl so frightened, and I wondered if he killed me what would happen to her. I tried to get those thoughts out of my head, I was more afraid for her than for myself. I closed my eyes and said a silent prayer no one else heard it but God. I said, "Dear God please I'm asking you to get me out of this situation alive, and I promise I will never pray to you to get me out of another situation with this man ever again because if I walk away, it will be forever this time." As soon as I was finished praying, I opened my eyes and instantly Monroe threw the knife into the kitchen sink. He punched me in my face with his fist then laughed out loudly as he walked away.

I picked Rebecca up hugged her tightly and told her I loved her very much. As I comforted her, I thought I must be just as crazy as he was to remain in this abusive relationship. The fear on Rebecca's face gave me the courage to leave him. This was not a healthy environment for her, and the sooner we left him the better off we would be. A stable life with one parent would be a thousand times better than living in a horrible violent environment with both parents. I sat there thinking of my escape, I knew I couldn't attempt to leave at that moment, because he would have prevented me from leaving and probably really hurt me this time. I pretended everything was ok, I put Rebecca to bed and I went to bed. Of course I couldn't fall asleep I was scared and I didn't know what was going through his screwed up mind either.

He had just started a new job he was working the night shift as a security guard. I was praying he would go to work because in instances like these he stayed at home. Surprisingly he left for work, and as soon as he was gone I got out of bed and packed a shopping bag full of clothes for Rebecca and a few things for myself. I left him a note it simply stated "do not come looking for me or Rebecca, I hate your fucking guts, I will never forgive you for this."

It was very late at night, going on midnight so I hurried up to catch the train since he had taken the car to work.

We took the train to Newark Penn then a cab to my mom's house in Orange NJ. It was almost midnight when we got there. By now my mom and I were back on speaking terms. She was surprised to see us there so late I told her what had happened, she was shocked she thought that everything was going well because I had stopped complaining to my family about him. I told her he was going to call or come here, and when he did to tell him she had not heard from me. I informed her we were just staying for the night, and the following day Rebecca and I would travel to Long Island to my cousin Linda, who was at home on maternity leave with her third child. She offered to take care of Rebecca until I found a baby sitter. Early the next morning he showed up at my mother's house looking for us and acting as though he was concerned for our well-being. She told him she had not heard from me, she was very concerned and asked him to call as soon as he heard anything. We left for Long Island it took us about three hours or more to get there. We took a cab to Newark Penn, then the NJ transit to NY Penn, and from there we took the LIRR to Ronkonkoma where Linda picked us up. I was very tired from the trip, but happy to be far away from him. I called my mom to let her know we had arrived safely.

I called my supervisor and informed him I needed an emergency leave of absence I told him exactly what was happening and where I was. He was very sympathetic and understanding to my cause, he told me not to worry and I should take whatever time I needed. He said my job would be there for me whenever I was ready to return to work. I stayed in Long Island for one week before returning to NJ, but I couldn't go back to my apartment because Monroe was still there. I went back to work and stayed with one of my co-workers, her name is Nadia. She was a very kind hearted person, a single parent with two little children and she too had been in similar situations in the past. I went back to city hall and filed another complaint against him for holding the knife to my throat and threatening to kill me again. A court date was set for thirty days from the date of filing the report. I pleaded with them to give me an earlier date, but I was told all domestic complaints were heard in thirty days.

Many years have gone by, and as I write tears still fill my eyes. I notified my landlord of the fact Rebecca and I were out of the apartment. I told them I wanted to keep the apartment and would continue to pay the rent but not to let Monroe know about my plans. At the end of the month he would have to leave because he couldn't afford to pay the rent. They agreed to this and I was able to secure my apartment and not have to move again.

I worked the evening shift three to eleven thirty p.m. and while at work one day, I received a phone call. When I answered the phone it was Monroe. He said thank God you are all right, I was looking all over for you, I was so nervous, I thought something might have happened to you. I didn't respond to his comments, I just put the phone back onto the receiver. I believe he followed us from work one night, he came to Nadia's apartment rang her door bell and asked for me. She told him if he didn't leave right then she would call the cops, so he left. After work one night we were leaving and heading towards the parking lot, as we exited the door someone grabbed my arm and started pulling me across the parking lot. It was Monroe he was hiding behind the door and I didn't see him I yelled out to Nadia to run back into the building to get security, when he saw her running back to get help he let go of my arm and sped off. I really was afraid for my life.

Finally the court date arrived, it was my first time in a court room I didn't know it was open court and everyone would hear your business. I was somewhat embarrassed. Our case was called and we both swore to tell the truth and nothing but the truth. The judge read my charges against him then he read his counter charges. His charges stated that I had pulled a knife on him, I was so shocked I couldn't believe my ears,

I'm sure the judge saw the look of disbelief on my face. After hearing all of my complaints and everything he'd done to me, the judge asked him to state his case. He was caught lying. He was found guilty of all charges, and he was also charged with perjury, this was a two hundred dollar fine which had to be paid on the spot or he'd be put in jail. He was given a restraining order and told he was not to come anywhere close to me. He did not have the two hundred dollars to pay, so he was locked up until his mother could get the money to take his sorry ass out. He had to vacate the apartment he took his clothes along with the car I had bought. I had paid seven hundred and fifty dollars for that car I let him have it I just wanted to get rid of him.

I moved back into the apartment and changed the locks on the door right away. I was looking for a babysitter for Rebecca, she was still in Long Island, I visited her on all of my days off, and every other weekend when I was off. I found a sitter who lived a few houses from me and Rebecca came back home after one month. I was so happy to bring her back home, and lucky to find a sitter so close to us. I bought a new car we needed that to make our lives easier. The restraining order did not stop Monroe from coming back to the apartment. The first time he came he tried to use his key, but I had changed the lock. He returned another time and broke the glass on the door I called the cops, and he took off. The landlord said that I had to pay for the repairs, I told them that I didn't break the glass and that they needed to get him to pay, they took him to court and made him pay for the damages. He was relentless, one day he visited my landlord and when he left he went out of their front door which brought him inside of the house to my apartment. He came up the stairs and put his key in my door and opened it, but the chain was on. In the meantime the landlord called to say what he had done. I picked up the phone and dialed 911. I told him that the cops were on their way, and he left. The landlord apologized and said that they would never let him in the house again. I was seriously considering moving out of state just to get away from him and his harassment. Crazy abusers do not acknowledge restraining orders, they don't care anything about the law, and they will go to all lengths to try to get to that woman, and many times, unfortunately they end up killing the woman or hurting her very badly, just because she wanted out of that abusive relationship.

My mom told me that Adrian my brother would be coming from Guyana to reside in the U.S. very shortly. She also said that she was looking for an apartment for him. I suggested that he stayed with us since I had a spare bedroom. Once Monroe realized that my brother was residing with us, the harassment of him showing up at my apartment stopped. He was a bully towards women, but would never stand up to another man. With Adrian there, I felt a lot more secured. I was also very happy that I had finally gotten rid of that bastard for good. There was peace and quiet in my home now, no more arguments or fights no one to wake me up in the middle of the night to start an argument or a fight.

My friends were advising me to go to court and file for custody for Rebecca. I thought that was nonsense, why do I need to file for custody for my own child. They explained to me that if he got the chance to take Rebecca from me like he once did, I would have to go through a lot of drama to get her back, and knowing that he was a nut job, I felt that he would do anything to hurt me because I had finally left him. So I listened to what my friends were telling me, I went to family court and filed for legal custody for Rebecca. This opened up a whole new can of worms. There were issues I would rather not have dealt with. I did not realize that along with custody, visitation and support were attached.

On the day of the hearing, I was sitting outside of the court room on a bench waiting for our case to be called. Monroe came in and sat on the bench next to me, so I moved over to the far end. He tried to speak to me, but I ignored him.

One of the office clerks came to me with some papers to fill out, and Monroe asked her if she knew of any marriage counselors who could help us work our problems out so that we could get back together. When he asked her that question, he was very polite, mannerly and soft spoken. His appearance to any stranger was sincerity and concern for his family. She looked at me and asked if we had any kids. I didn't answer her, but Monroe said yes we have a beautiful little daughter. The clerk said that she didn't know of any marriage counselors, but she would try to get that information for us. She looked directly at me and said you should try to work things out with your husband, especially for your daughter's sake, he seems like such a nice man. I lost it. I said to her lady please don't waste your time looking up information on marriage counselors, I'm done when I wanted to try counseling he wasn't interested now I'm definitely not interested. I said it in a nasty tone, she looked at me as though I was the guilty one, but I didn't give a damn.

Our case was called the Judge asked each of us about our professions and how much money we made. I offered my information to the judge, and Monroe told him that he was currently unemployed. The judge asked him where he was residing he told him that he was living with his mother at the present time. The judge asked about child care, I told him that Rebecca had a baby sitter. The decision was made, I was granted full custody he was given visitation rights, and ordered to pay twenty-five dollars in child support weekly.

I was happy about the fact that I was granted full custody, but I was really upset over the fact that he was given visitation rights. The child support I couldn't care less about I didn't need his lousy twenty-five dollars a week, he never paid it anyway. The plan was for him to see Rebecca every Wednesday, and every other weekend for two hours each day until she started school. That meant that he would have to come back to the apartment to see her that was my biggest concern.

He showed up every-time on visitation days, he never missed a beat. Whenever he came to see her, he gave Rebecca hugs and kisses and played with her for a few minutes then he'd tell her to go play with her toys. The rest of time he dedicated to me. He tried to have conversations with me, most of the time I ignored him, and I kept reminding him that he was there to see Rebecca and not me.

During one of his visits, I was at the kitchen sink he sat on a chair in the kitchen and played with Rebecca for a few minutes, his usual quality time he spent with her. Then he told her to go and play with her toys. I was busy washing dishes, but I could see from my peripheral view that he was looking at me. I turned my head towards him, and his eyes were plastered on my ass, I guess my pants were too tight as he used to say. I stared him down for at least five minutes before he realized that I was looking at him. He jumped when he realized that I was looking at him, it seemed as though he was in a trance that was a very scary moment for me. I told him to get out of my apartment right now before I call the cops he left peacefully.

Another time he came and started looking through my clothes closet he was looking for men's clothing. He'd always play with Rebecca for five minutes then he'd try to occupy my time with him even if it was in a negative manner. I was still afraid of him, but I would not let him know that. Many times I organized to have a male family member to be in the apartment while he visited that was the only way I had peace, but it wasn't always possible to have someone there. Every time he came to visit I had to throw him out after the two hours were up he never left on his own. Many times I threatened to call the cops to get him out, once he refused to leave, so I grabbed Rebecca and ran out of the apartment, he stayed up there for about half an hour I had no clue what he was doing in there probably looking through my clothes again. Eventually he came downstairs, and when he did I ran through the door and locked it behind me.

I took him back to court to change the visitation arrangements I couldn't have him come to my apartment anymore it was not working out, I knew that it wouldn't work out, but I always give people the benefit of the doubt. The judge reviewed my complaints, and he revised the order. He was allowed to take her every Wednesday and every other weekend, but she had to be back home by six p.m. It broke my heart to send Rebecca with him, but that decision was out of my control, all I could do was pray that she'd be ok. I did stay in touch with his family, because through-out all of this, they were always very good to me. I knew that when he took her that she would be at his mother's house, and that gave me some peace of mind. One day when he brought her back, she started telling me something at first I didn't understand what she was saying, because she was saying it very fast and over and over again. Finally I got it she was saying mommy and daddy together again, she sounded like a little parrot, that son of a bitch drilled that into her head to tell me when she got home. I guessed he thought that I would fall for that crap and get back with him I guess he really didn't know me either.

Every time she came back from weekends with her dad, I questioned her about the events of her weekend. She'd always tell me who she saw and where he took her. Monroe and his girlfriend had a new baby boy he was born nine months to the date that he and I separated. His girlfriend's name was Flora I was very happy for him, having another family meant that he would leave me alone.

On Rebecca's return home one day, she seemed to be very nervous when I asked her what happened on the weekend, she said nothing happened. I asked if she stayed by her daddy's girlfriend or by her grandmother, she said that she stayed by her grandmother. I asked her why she didn't stay by his girlfriend's house she said that Flora was very mean to her. I asked her what she did she told me that her daddy took her to Flora's house because she had to use the bathroom, but when they got there, Flora refused to open the door even though her daddy told her that she had to use the bathroom. So I asked her what happened next, she told me that her daddy kicked in Flora's door. That's all I needed to hear as far as I was concerned, his rights to visitation were over. I was not going to continue to have my daughter exposed to his madness. Every time she came back from those weekends with him, she always seemed to be out of sorts it always took a few days before she'd settle back in. That was it for me, I was done I decided then and there that she would not be going back anywhere with him ever. I called him up and told him that he shouldn't come back to get her anymore, I told him that I was taking him back to court, that he was an unfit father, and I was going to have his visitation rights revoked.

I wrote a letter to the judge who presided in our custody hearings. I told him about all of the incidences that occurred whenever she was in his presence. I asked him to please revoke his visitation rights, because I felt that he was not providing a nurturing and healthy environment for Rebecca while she was with him. I did inform him that the reason I left Monroe was because of the same abusive behaviors he had towards me, and I did not want Rebecca to grow up in the midst of this all the time. I told him that I would not be sending Rebecca back with her dad anymore for weekend visits. I sent Monroe a copy of the letter I sent to the judge. A few weeks later I received a response from the judge, he wrote that I had some valid reasons and concerns for Rebecca's wellbeing, but that I couldn't take it into my own hands to stop visitation. He suggested that I take Monroe back to court and present my case, and he would make a decision. I had enough of family court, I was tired of fighting him, I never took him back to court neither did I ever send her back with him for any more weekend visitation, that was the end of that.

I received a call from Melba one of Monroe's nieces, she told me that her uncle had broken his girlfriend's arm. She said that he wanted to take her car and she refused, she grabbed her keys and she wouldn't give it up, so he twisted her arm until he broke it and she dropped the keys. Her arm was in a cast I guess it must have been difficult taking care of a new born baby while one arm was casted. That was no longer my problem that clearly belonged to someone else.

Divorce

I consulted with a divorce lawyer, who advised me that I should write down all of the abusive encounters I had with Monroe and present it to the court. He told me that if I did that, my divorce would be granted immediately and I wouldn't have to wait for the recommended time after filing. Every-time I started writing out those encounters, they stirred up so many unpleasant emotions and hateful feelings, that I had to stop. Several months passed, and I wasn't able to write out those abusive encounters, I just filed the divorce papers and waited for the appropriate time. The court date was set, Monroe showed up with his mother he had no attorney. The case was called I was represented by my attorney, everything went in my favor, I was granted the divorce, visitation rights were once again set, and he was ordered to pay the same twenty five dollars per week for child support, the only difference this time was that he would have to pay it through the courts. He did for a short while, but then he stopped I never pursued that, because some-things are better left alone.

Whenever people ask me if I have forgiven Monroe for all the things he has done to me, I always say that I would like to think that I have forgiven him, but I'm not so sure, especially when I can never forget the way he treated me. I never deserved any of that I have always been a good person, all I wanted was to have a loving and peaceful family life, and he made sure that I didn't have that with him. To this day I know one thing for sure, and that is I cannot stand to be anywhere near him, I cannot stand the sight of him, it's almost as though I despise him, and with that being said, I guess that I truly have not forgiven him. One thing I know for sure is that I have not allowed his abuse to keep me from moving on with my life. It has actually helped me to become a stronger person in all aspects of life, and once when I saw him, I said I would like to thank you, he said for what and I said for the son of a bitch you have turned me into, and I walked away.

Later on I found out that Monroe grew up in an abusive environment. His mother told me that her husband was abusive towards her, that he'd always hit her and was a very jealous man who always accused her wrongfully of having affairs. I asked her what did she do about it and why didn't she leave him. She said that every time he hit her she went and sat outside until he calmed down and then she went back into the house. Monroe was the youngest of six children I guess she felt stuck in her situation. She stayed with him until he died of a massive heart attack while he was only in his forties. Monroe was practicing what he saw growing up as a child, in his warped mind he thought that was normal behavior, and that I also would put up with his abuse forever. This apparently was the reason she kept telling Monroe while I was pregnant that a man should never hit a pregnant woman, I didn't understand it then but now I know that she had valid reasons for telling him that. Monroe's abusive behaviors towards me didn't surface until after Rebecca's birth, I guess that he couldn't wait. Instead of her telling him you should never hit a pregnant woman, she should have told him that you should never hit any woman ever.

When Rebecca started Kindergarten, I enrolled her into the neighborhood dance academy which she enjoyed very much, taking ballet, jazz and tap dancing. Later on I enrolled her in piano classes, this she hated. I was busy driving Rebecca back and forth to her after school activities. I was skeptical of starting relationships my level of trust was way down, and honestly I had no desire to get involved with anyone. I had no time for socialization, I worked full time and I had to take care of Rebecca making sure that all of her needs were met. I tried to make up for all of the turmoil she went through during her first two and one half years of life. My life was good I took Rebecca with me every place I went. I showered her with toys I made sure that she never needed anything.

Shaka

I really enjoyed working the day shift it brought a normalcy to my life, I worked on the med-surg unit, and somehow all of the psych patients were admitted to our unit. It was a small community hospital with about three hundred beds. There was a prison in the next town over, so whenever prisoners became ill they were sent to our hospital, and they too were always admitted to our unit. Sometimes there were as many as three prisoners hospitalized at the same time, and for each prisoner there were two correction officers. I had a prisoner as one of my patients he was very sick and was hospitalized for a long time. One of the officers who guarded him started talking to me, I never said anything to any of them, but I noticed that some of the female employees always came to our unit whenever we had prisoners just to see and flirt with the officers. Each time that officer came to the unit he'd ask me how I was doing, then one day he said that they were about to order and he offered to buy me lunch. I looked at him with a smile and hesitantly said oh thank you. He was actually very handsome. He knew my name already because of my hospital ID he told me that his name was Shaka Zulu I looked at him and started laughing that broke the ice. He actually was built like Shaka Zulu, except I had never taken the time to notice. It was apparent that he frequented the gym and took excellent care of himself.

We exchanged phone numbers and started calling each other. He worked the evening shift at the prison, and he gave me his work number. I decided that I wanted to get to know him better and would like to go out with him. We went out to eat a few times and actually enjoyed each other's company. I told him that I had a little girl and I was newly divorced from a horrible marriage and that I was skeptical about relationships. He told me that he also had a little girl, but that he was still married to this miserable woman, and he was still there because of his little girl. I made the decision to continue seeing him, I thought that was the perfect situation since I was not looking for a husband any time soon, I thought that would be the perfect arrangement.

I convinced myself that it didn't matter that he was a married man. I guess my self-esteem had hit rock bottom, and I was just thinking about myself at that moment and not on a long term basis and the consequences that may occur. We worked conflicting shifts. He worked evenings and I worked the day shift, by the time he got off duty I was already in bed. Our dates consisted mostly of him visiting me at midnight when he got off work, and leaving after a few hours of steamy love making, and once in a while we went out on actual dates. He would have been the perfect gentleman had he been single. He was funny, had a good sense of humor, very intelligent and knew how to treat a lady. We had a lot in common, I liked being with him he always made me feel loved. We didn't always agree on everything, but there was never an issue with abuse or bullying. He made me aware that there are really good men out there, they are not all monsters.

My problem was that he belonged to someone else and every-time he visited he always had to leave to go home. This affair went on for a few years sometimes he called me from his home at nights, and we spoke on the phone for eternity. I was so in love with him, apparently that clouded my judgment. One day I received a phone call from a woman, who claimed that she was a telephone operator and that someone by the name of Shaka wanted to make a collect call. I didn't fall for that, because he never called collect, I said I didn't know anyone by that name, and I wouldn't accept the call and hung up. She called right back and said the same thing, I hung up again. The same woman called back a few days later and asked me my name. I said who are you and why are you calling, she said that her name was Mari and that Shaka was her husband, and she wanted to know how I knew him. I said woman you must have the wrong number I don't know anyone by that name, and I would appreciate it if you didn't call this number anymore. She continued to call my phone every day and I always hung up on her. One day she called and I was not in a good mood, so I decided that I would take care of her for once and for all. She told me that she knew that I was fucking her man, and that I had aids. HIV was the newest sexually transmitted disease of that time. She kept talking a whole lot of crap. I told her that I had enough I said now you shut up and listen to me. I said if I am fucking your man and I have aids, then you stupid bitch, you have it too. Do not call this fucking number anymore, and I hung up. That was the last time I heard from her.

My aunt Olga was visiting with my mom, and one day when I returned from work she told me that a female named Mari called and said that she was a friend of mine, but she hadn't heard from me in a while, she wanted to know how I was doing, and she needed my address so she can send me a card. My dear aunty gave that bitch my address, thinking that she was really a friend of mine. I was so upset with her, but I tried to hide it, I just told her that I didn't have any friends by that name, and that she should not give my address out to anyone else again. I immediately got in touch with Shaka and told him what happened. We had to be very cautious about seeing each other since she knew where I lived, and there was a very strong possibility she could have him followed. That put a damper on things between us, so we decided to slow things down for a while. I was hurting though because I was in love with this man and he belonged to someone else, I knew that it was wrong and that I was being selfish but I couldn't help it. We continued the relationship, but I started to realize that even though I said in the beginning that all I wanted was friendship, this was not the case. Shaka always told me that he and his wife did not have a good relationship, he always said that she was a miserable bitch and the only reason he stayed was because of his little girls. One day we were talking and I realized that he had been honest with me all along he never said that he would leave his wife, and I knew that I wanted more, I wanted him all to myself or nothing, I was not going to live that life anymore he belonged to someone else. I felt that it was wrong I didn't want to be the reason for breaking up someone's marriage, so I decided that we should call it quits, it was getting to be too complicated.

Our conclusion was to stop seeing each other for a while, to play it safe. That was very difficult it was tearing me apart. We spoke on the phone, and on a few occasions we got together. Eventually I decided that this wasn't working for me, and knew that it was time to really stop the madness. I told Shaka that we needed to end our relationship, that as much as I loved him, I had to let go because I had finally come to the realization and accepted the fact that he belonged to someone else. Our decision was final, but we remained friendly since neither one of us really wanted to say goodbye. We had a very good relationship and friendship, and always enjoyed each other's company and conversations. He was a gentleman and treated me like a lady all of the time. After our mutually agreed upon breakup, we stayed in touch, with occasional phone calls to see how each other was doing. Every holiday I received a call from him wishing me greetings, for that holiday, and to touch base with each other.

My True Identity

One day I received a letter from an attorney it was about the station master Mr. B who had recently suffered a massive heart attack and died. The letter listed all of his assets, and all of his children there were fourteen names listed, and low and behold to my surprise I saw the name Adrianna Rose, I was in disbelief and shock, I was listed as one of Mr. B's children I couldn't believe what I was seeing. I read that letter over and over again trying to understand and digest this information. My first thought was to confront my mom with this letter, but I realized that I was too angry to approach her, I was afraid that if I confronted her at that time, that we'd probably end up not speaking to each other again. I called my aunt Precious Pearl and my aunty Olga and asked each one of them if they knew that Mr. B was my dad, I told them about the letter I had received from the attorney with my name listed as one of his children. They both were very evasive and neither one of them ever admitted the fact that they knew this, they both told me that I should speak to my mom. I never asked her, I guess I realized that it was a very difficult subject to approach, and I knew that I didn't want to hurt her feelings, so I forever left it alone. I then accepted the fact that he indeed was my father, and I also realized that was the reason he was always so kind to me when I was a young child back in Guyana, and that my very good friend Kathryn and her brothers and sisters were also my brothers and sisters. The funny thing is that they all knew that I was their sister all along, but none of them ever told me. Maybe they thought I knew that they were my brothers and sisters. My mom kept this very important information from me until she died, I will never understand why she didn't tell me who my real dad was, there were so many instances when she could have said something to me. I was in my late thirties when I found out through the lawyer's letter and it wasn't until he too had passed away, how sad. Looking back, when my friend Ona had told me that Mr. B. was my dad, I should have listened to her and taken it a step further and investigated. All of those years I thought that my brother Adrian and I had the same mom and dad and that he was my only sibling. I have never officially said anything to Adrian about this myself but soon enough he'll find out. That was my letter of confirmation from my dad's attorney of my true identity.

My First Home

After living in the apartment in that old house for eleven years, I bought a cape cod it was cozy and charming. It had three bedrooms on the first floor, two bedrooms on the second floor, and a full finished basement. It was appropriate for us, my mom was living with us, she was having problems with the same people she went to work for when I asked her to come and live with us and she said no. Now she was not happy with the working situation, and she asked me if she could come and stay with us and I told her yes. I had forgiven her for not helping us out when we really needed her. It was fun having my own home, I bought Rebecca a puppy she always wanted a dog. The first week after she got the puppy, she got up early every morning to walk him. That lasted exactly one week.

Every summer we took a vacation and traveled either out of state or out of the country. When Rebecca was six years old we went to Barbados for a week we had a grand time. We went on a party boat and there was a dance contest, there were the child and adult categories, Rebecca won the children's category and I won the adult category. I always tried to give Rebecca the best of everything, I tried to compensate for her not having both parents I didn't want her to feel deprived of anything.

Rebecca was growing up, she was very beautiful, she attended private school, and she was involved in a lot of extra-curricular activities. I was very busy taking her back and forth to her activities. Rebecca has a lot of artistic talents, which I always tried to encourage. After she graduated elementary school, she attended a private all girl's high school.

The Pageant

At age fifteen I encouraged Rebecca to participate in a teenage pageant it was the NJ'S perfect teen pageant at first she didn't want to, but with some coaxing she decided that she would enter. I told Rebecca that it was a good thing to do especially since she had interests in the arts, and this would be an excellent experience for her. I encouraged her to just have fun, and not to put any pressure on herself about the outcome. Being chosen out of hundreds of girls throughout the state in it-self was an honor we took care of all of the preliminaries in preparation for the pageant which was held in Cherry Hill. It was held over a two day weekend, and there were eighty four young ladies who participated in the pageant. Their ages ranged from thirteen to nineteen, Rebecca was fifteen years old at the time.

The first day they wore navy blue shorts with white short-sleeved polo shirts and red scarfs. Each young lady was assigned a number Rebecca was 34. They introduced themselves by telling the audience their names, age, and where they were from. When Rebecca came out, she said hello my name is Rebecca Rose I'm fifteen years old, and I'm from Rahway NJ. Her smile was radiant and she said it with conviction, she looked beautiful. After all of the introductions were completed, the contestants returned to the dressing rooms to change into their evening gowns. They all looked very beautiful. Of course Rebecca was stunning. The judges asked all of the contestants questions about themselves, and they all seemed to do well. The first day concluded with every one anxiously waiting for the next day of final competition.

We were all happy excited and nervous. We got up early the following day and got ready for the pageant. We had breakfast and just waited around the hotel lobby. Rebecca came into the lobby with some of the contestants we hugged, and wished her good luck then they left to get ready for the finale. We had a large group of family members she had both of her grandmothers, many aunts, uncles and cousins to cheer her on, it was about thirteen of us there. I was such a wreck, I told everyone in our group that we had to get there very early, so as to secure front seats, which we did.

The contestants were presented once again in their red white and blue sportswear. They changed into their evening gowns and were introduced to the audience as they walked down the stage. Each contestant was escorted by a member of the JROTC. Rebecca wore a strapless white evening gown, that fitted tightly across her chest and waist which flowed into a full skirt, with sequins on the top and front of the dress. The dress had a very large bow in the back at the waist line. It was tailored to fit Rebecca perfectly. Her hair was done in a bun with some hair coming down the left side of her face. She was elegant. After all of the questions and answers, it was time for choosing the ten finalists.

They started calling out the names of the finalists I was very nervous, and just hoping that Rebecca's name would be called. I would truly be proud to say that she was one of the ten finalists. Out of eighty-four girls, Rebecca was one of the ten finalists we were all very happy and cheering loudly. There were more questions and answers for the ten finalists, Rebecca did very well with her answers, she never appeared to be nervous as she maintained her composure with that beautiful dimpled million dollar smile. Out of that ten, five were chosen Rebecca was in that final five, this was getting to be very serious, we were cheering very loudly, I think that we were one of the largest and loudest groups.

There were more interviews, and each one of the five finalists was given a red rose in their hands, as the master of ceremony sang the song unforgettable to each one of them. This was truly beautiful. I was sitting on the edge of my chair, and I was now looking at all of the other contestants, wondering which one of them could win this pageant. Actually they were all very beautiful I felt my heart racing. My niece Chemy was sitting next to me, she has always been a very emotional person. She told me that she was nervous, she was crying and hyperventilating. She told me that she was having difficulty breathing I put my arms around her and told her to calm down and take slow deep breaths. I kept trying to keep her calm, then I told her that if she didn't stop I would have to take her outside and that if I missed the show I would kill her, she started laughing and got it together. By then they had named the second runner up, then the first runner up, there were three girls still standing there and Rebecca was one of them all waiting in suspense.

We were all holding our breaths and finally the master of ceremony said "and the winner of the 1995 NJ perfect teen pageant is number 34, Miss Rebecca Rose." Oh my God we all screamed, we jumped out of our seats, I was jumping up and down and screaming, I couldn't believe it, I was saying that's my daughter and she won the title. We were very loud Rebecca was crying the outgoing winner put the red sash with the title NJ Perfect Teen across her gown, and then she crowned her with that beautiful tiara. The M.C. looked over to where we were celebrating and he said to Rebecca I guess that's your family over there, with a smile she said can you tell and he laughed. Rebecca took her victory walk waving to the audience, she looked absolutely stunning. We were all taking pictures after the ceremony, I was hoarse from screaming, the next day was Monday, I stayed home from work, and I kept Rebecca home from school, after that she deserved a day off from school. She was very happy. She was a sophomore in high school. Rebecca was a good kid, we were always very close and we had a good relationship.

Kendrick

She came into the G.I. lab and asked for me then she introduced herself as Iris. She said I'm an employee here and I work on a medical unit on the third floor and someone told me you're from Guyana. I wanted to meet you, because I am also from Guyana. We talked for a while, and eventually we became friends. She had connections with people in New York who were involved in social activities with the Guyanese community. She often invited me to events, but I always came up with excuses why I couldn't attend. She invited me to a dance which was held yearly by members of her church, on the Friday after thanksgiving. It was November of 1995. This was a fund raising event, and the tickets were fifty dollars each. I purchased a few tickets and invited my cousin Dawn and her friend Eric. Iris wanted to introduce me to a male friend of hers on the night of the dance, and I agreed. As the time got closer to the event I wanted to change my mind but I couldn't because I had already invited Dawn and her friend and they were all excited about going.

After we arrived at the dance, Iris informed me her friend couldn't make it, but there was someone else she wanted to introduce to me. She returned to our table accompanied by a tall, slim, handsome young man who appeared to be very personable. She said Adrianna I would like you to meet my friend Kendrick. I looked up at him, shook his hand and we both exchanged smiles. I introduced him to Dawn and Eric, and invited him to sit with us. We all had fun talking and dancing, it was a great event, and I was very happy I had made the decision to attend the dance. Kendrick and Eric connected immediately and they exchanged their experiences about living in Guyana. At the conclusion of the event, Kendrick and I exchanged phone numbers before leaving.

The following day I called Dawn to go over the events of the night before. I asked her opinion of Kendrick and voiced some concerns. I told her he had already called in the morning, and when I asked his age, I was stunned by his reply. He was younger and I didn't know what to say. I was silent for a moment then I told him my age and said we should not go any further with this. His reply was age is just a number, and I don't have an issue with the age difference. I said I do have an issue with this. I asked Dawn for her opinion on this issue, and she said what the hell if you like him you should give him a chance and take it from there. We continued calling each other, but the age difference continued to bug me. Mainly because I worried about what people would say. Then I thought what the hell if we really like each other, it shouldn't matter what other people think. If it was the other way around this would not be an issue. I've always been told I look younger than my actual age. We went out on several dates, we both loved dancing and enjoyed being with each other. I introduced Kendrick to my mom and Rebecca my mom immediately liked him I guess because he was very friendly, but Rebecca appeared to be reserved.

Ken had only been in the U.S. for a short period of time when we met. He and his younger brother Ray had recently joined the rest of their family who had migrated from Guyana several years earlier. Ken wanted to introduce me to his family, so one Sunday he asked me to go with him to Brooklyn to meet them. When we arrived there were several family members gathered they included his mother, his oldest sister, his youngest brother Ray, and some of his nieces and nephews. I walked into the apartment after Ken and he introduced me to his family. I said hello to everyone, but his mother and oldest sister both looked at me without responding. Their facial expressions were not very welcoming and they both turned away without acknowledging my presence. His brother Ray and niece Lea started a conversation with me, it was apparent they were embarrassed about the situation and they were trying to ease the tension. They were about to have dinner and Ken asked me if I would join them. I said no thank you I would rather leave now. As soon as we got into the car I asked him if he had noticed the looks I received from his mother and sister, he admitted he did and said he would speak to his mother about her rude behavior.

The following Sunday we visited his other sister Kristy she greeted me and made me feel comfortable. While we were talking the doorbell rang and two women walked in, it was obvious they had just come from church. The first one through the door was Ken's mother when she saw me she stared me down and turned her face away without saying anything as she walked past me. The other woman came over and introduced herself to me, she said I'm Ken's aunt and my name is Ruby I said my name is Adrianna and it's a pleasure to meet you. Kristy called her mother out right in front of me, she said mom you came into the house and you saw Adrianna sitting there and you passed her by without saying hello that's not very polite, and you just came from church. She still did not speak to me, and after we left I asked Ken what was his mother's problem and what was her reason for not speaking to me. He said he didn't know, I decided I would keep my distance from her.

I heard through the grape vine Ken's mom told someone she didn't like me because I was older than Ken, and if it was the last thing she did it would be to make sure Ken left me. I told her to tell his mom she could do whatever the hell she wished, because I didn't need anything from Ken. I said please make her aware that I am an educated, independent and professional woman, who had been taking care of myself before I met her son and I don't depend on anyone for anything. Every time Ken visited her I waited in the car until he came back out.

His sister Kristy is a socialite she is well known within the Guyanese community in Brooklyn. She invited us to many social functions and every weekend we were kept very busy attending events. A few months later Ken had almost completely moved in. This made his mom very upset and she told someone it seemed as though I was so badly in need of a man, I was going after her son who is younger than I am. She wanted to know what kind of woman I was to be going after a younger man. This pissed me off and I asked who does she think she is to be talking about me in this manner and as a matter of fact her son was the one who pursued the relationship. My social life was rejuvenated after I met Ken I was once again doing things I enjoyed and having much fun with him.

Graduation

Rebecca's high school graduation was soon approaching there were lots of planning going on. First it was preparations for the prom, Rebecca wore a beautiful green and silver gown which she sketched and designed all by herself, and had a designer make. She was involved in choosing and purchasing the material. It turned out to be beautiful. On the day of the prom I invited a few close friends and family to our home for a celebration I decorated the house with green and silver balloons and streamers to match Rebecca's gown. I rented a stretch limo for Rebecca and her date, they were the only couple in the limo, I wanted her to have a Cinderella type of experience I didn't want her to have to share the limo with other kids. Of course Rebecca looked stunning in her green and silver gown with silver high heeled sandals and accessories.

Rebecca graduated high school in May of 1996 the graduation ceremony was beautiful. It was held outdoors, and luckily the day was sunny and bright. The girls all wore white gowns and caps. After the ceremony we headed home where there were preparations for a very large BBQ with all of the family and friends. We all had lots to eat and drink and we all had a grand time.

That summer I took Rebecca to Georgetown Guyana that was her graduation gift. I wanted her to see where I grew up, I had taken her there once before, I wanted my grandmother to meet her, she was only about three years old, she couldn't remember much if anything about it. I took my mom with us that was her last visit to Guyana. She stayed with my God mother Winnie, while Rebecca and I stayed with my sister Kathryn and her husband Derrick we had a grand time. Rebecca did not want to come back home, because she was having such good times with her cousins, they took her to clubs every night, that was a privilege she didn't have at home. My brother in law Derrick took us on his speed boat to his farm in the country for a day of fun. The farm was massive there were lots of cattle and other farm animals. There was a very large farm house with a hammock on the front porch Rebecca and I kept fighting each other for time in the hammock. Derrick grilled, we had plenty to eat and drink, including lots of fresh coconut water right off the tree. It was dark when we left to go back to the city, I was a little nervous to get on the boat, but I tried not to show it. We were there for three weeks.

After we came back, it was time to get ready for Rebecca to go away to college. That was very difficult for me, because it was just Rebecca and I for such a long time, she is my only child, and she was getting ready to leave the nest. Rebecca was ready to leave, she wanted her independence looking back I do believe that I was one of those overbearing parent, I protected her from the harshness of life I didn't want her to get caught up with the wrong crowd, so just like my grandmother raised me, I tried to raise her.

When the time came we loaded up the car and drove to Pennsylvania that drive was about an hour and a half away. We helped Rebecca to unpack and get settled in. The campus was very beautiful it had a vast landscape with large trees manicured lawns and beautiful buildings, and most importantly it was in a very safe community, that was my number one priority. When I returned home, that's when reality set in I started wondering how I was going to make it without her and at the same time wondering if Rebecca missed home as much as I missed her. I missed taking her back and forth to all of her after school activities my life was just about to become boring, I was definitely feeling the empty nest syndrome. I worried a lot about her, how she would manage her schedule without me there by her side constantly helping her out. I was already looking forward to our first visit to her campus, and her first trip back home on break.

Ken and I planned weekend activities and we were always doing something, even if it just meant going over to the city to shop in china town, or stroll through the village, which was always a lot of fun to see all of the different personalities, there's no place like New York City. Ken had actually moved in by now, and he was constantly proposing to me, which I kept rejecting mainly because of the age difference. Rebecca came home on holidays and semester breaks. One weekend we all went over to the city to visit my cousin Dawn and her family, Ken and I had made reservations for an evening cruise on the World Yacht around Manhattan island it was a wonderful evening and after dinner Ken pulled a small box from his pocket and in it was a beautiful engagement ring he proposed and I accepted. We were both very happy. When we got back to Dawn's place I showed everyone the engagement ring, and they were all very happy. Later on, someone told me that Rebecca said that she didn't like Ken, and she hoped that our relationship didn't last.

Rebecca became rebellious and went against everything I said. We had many arguments I couldn't believe she was the same person at times. I reminded Rebecca no matter what happened no one would ever replace the love I have for her. I made her aware I have the right to happiness, and to be with whomever I wanted to be with. Ken and I were receiving negative vibes from both sides of the family. This created stressful situations in our relationship.

Chapel By The Sea

We had planned our summer vacation at the end of August for Myrtle Beach South Carolina. I had gone there once before when Rebecca was a contestant in a national pageant, and had fallen in love with the place, and always wanted to go back there. I didn't want to have a traditional wedding I just wanted to go to the justice of peace, but this was Ken's first time to be married, and he wanted something more than that. I compromised and made arrangements to have the ceremony in the chapel by the sea in Myrtle Beach. I made all necessary arrangements with the city hall to obtain our marriage licenses. I told my mom about our plans to get married in Myrtle Beach, and of course she was very happy for us. Ken asked his oldest brother Isaac to be his best man and he agreed. We took Rebecca and my niece Kenya with us to Myrtle Beach, we drove there from N.J., and Isaac flew down to meet us there. No one else knew about our plans. We rented a condo on the beach, it was very spacious and the scenery was beautiful.

The limousine arrived, we all got into it, and it sped off to the chapel by the sea where the ceremony was performed. Our witnesses were Rebecca and Isaac, the chapel was nicely decorated. It had all of the trimmings of a wedding ceremony, it was beautiful. We had arranged for a photographer and a videographer, everything was well coordinated. After we took our vows, the minister said "I pronounce you man and wife, you may kiss the bride." We signed the certificates took pictures, and when everything was completed at the chapel, the limo took us back to the condo. We danced had a little champagne then took off to a sea food restaurant that had been highly recommended. The food was excellent we all had a great time. Isaac flew back home the following day, while we stayed on for the remainder of the week. We visited museums, amusement parks and we went canoeing at the hard rock cafe. We all had a very good time. When we returned home, we had a big surprise for all of the folks here. Rumors were spreading like wild fire, some of Ken's family members were very upset, especially his mother, I had done a bad thing I had taken her son away from her and married him. The relationship between her and I remained strained for a very long time, it was almost none existent, but eventually we became tolerant of each other and have since built a relationship.

Life was good, we bought a jeep a Toyota 4 Runner, the color was purple my favorite color. At first I was a bit skeptical about driving the jeep, it seemed so high, I had Ken ride with me the first few times I took it out, and after that there was no stopping me. When I met Ken, I was working at the hospital in the town I lived in. My commute to work was two minutes away which was very convenient, I really liked working there. Before I met Ken I worked a lot of overtime, and my life style was a reflection of the money I made.

Financial Difficulties

Many of the hospitals started experiencing financial difficulties, they decided to have cut backs to save the hospital money any way they could. Overtime was one of the ways they decided to cut back on. This affected me tremendously, I had become dependent on that money, after the overtime was cut, my salary was decreased about fourteen hundred dollars monthly. I was experiencing serious financial difficulties. I had ran up large amounts of credit cards debt, and taken out a home equity loan to pay off my bills a few years earlier. I went right back and maxed out those cards again. My credit was plunging so fast, there was no way I could keep up with my first mortgage, a home equity loan, maxed out credit cards, parent loan, and all of the other bills I had. I did not tell Ken about any of this for a long time, because I felt that I had gotten myself into this mess, and I was determined to get out of it all by myself. I tried to keep up with the bills, but soon it just got to be too much. I was late with my payments, the credit card companies kept calling it got to the point where I was afraid to answer my phone. I was overwhelmed.

I was talking with my cousin Linda, and told her that I was swamped in bills, and I didn't know how I could ever manage to get a grip on my finances again. She told me that she knew of a program that could help me she assured me that it worked, since she herself was a current member of that program. She gave me the info and I called the company. The company's name was RRS, I was told that I had to be at least three months behind in my mortgage payments before I could be considered for the program, I thought no problem, since I was already two months behind. I was told the way it works, is that I would have to start making partial monthly payments to this company, and after one year the company will negotiate with the mortgage company to repurchase my home. Reluctantly I enrolled in the program, it was March of 1998. There were lots of legal forms and contracts to sign, I did all of the necessary paperwork, my mortgage payment was almost fifteen hundred dollars monthly, and I was asked to pay this rescue program thirteen hundred dollars monthly. I was informed to stop making payments on all other obligations, and was promised guidance throughout the program. The creditors kept calling, and I kept dodging them, then sometimes I'd send a payment just to keep them quiet for a while. I followed Linda's progress very carefully, she seemed very confident in how she was progressing. I kept making my monthly payments on time and stayed in touch with the company to know how my situation was coming along.

At the end of the first year, I thought that my problems would soon be over, and that everything would be just fine and dandy. Frankie assured me that everything was moving right along as planned, and that I needed to continue making my payments, since that was the most important aspect of the program. I continued with the payments, all the while wondering what would be the outcome. Linda called one day and told me that she had heard from the company, and her deal was about to be closed. The way the program worked was by allowing the homes to go into foreclosure buying the homes back from the bank and selling it back to the person. She seemed to be very nervous, on the day of the sale she was accompanied by one of their representatives to the sheriff's sale, she called me when she got home, and told me that it was over. They had purchased her home, and she would soon buy it back from them.

This gave me hope and I began to feel better, knowing that soon my time will come and I would be able to keep my house. In the mean time I was receiving registered mail from the mortgage company stating that my house was in foreclosure. I also received letters from the second mortgage company, with threats to garnish my check. I was very upset over these issues I called Frankie and informed him of what was happening. He had me mail copies of all the correspondence to him, and whatever he did, he was able to stop them from garnishing my check. He was also able to stop the foreclosure process at that time. My confidence was beginning to build with him.

In May of 1999 I received my tax return check for over five thousand dollars which I deposited into my checking account, and paid my bills. I attempted to make a small purchase with my debit card, but it was denied. I had the cashier swipe the card two more times with the same outcome it was late in the evening so I couldn't do anything until the next day. The following day I went to the bank, this was Saturday morning I spoke to the manager who ran a check on my account, she said I'm very sorry, but someone has put a lean on your account. I asked her who had put the lean on my account she couldn't tell me. I told her that I had written out a lot of checks and had already mailed them out. I asked her what would happen she said that more than likely the checks would bounce, because the bank could not release the money. I was devastated, what can I do now, all of those checks were about to bounce. I called Frankie immediately, I was frantic he told me that he would get back to me soon. When he called back, he gave me the name of an attorney, and told me that I should go and see him, and the company would pay the attorney's fees. The attorney told me that the lean was put on by the second mortgage company, and that legally they're not allowed to do that. He informed me that he would resolve the problem and the money would be released back to me. In the meantime all of the checks were returning and the bank was charging me thirty two dollars for each check they didn't care anything about the circumstances. The money was tied up, and would be tied up for a while until this battle was resolved. The bills were still unpaid and I was in one huge mess.

Every pay day I took my check to a check cashing place where I purchased money orders to pay my bills. This was a very embarrassing situation for me, I felt out of sorts. This went on for a few months, and eventually the situation was resolved in my favor. The bank had to release the money back to me, but I still had to pay the bank fees for all of those returned checks. That cost me a couple hundred dollars. Once that was all cleared up, I opened up another checking account with a different bank.

I received a call from Frankie informing me that I needed to go to the state capital to the court house to file bankruptcy. I asked him if that was necessary, he said that everything was coming to a close, and that I needed to do this to keep the second mortgage company and the other creditors from filing law suits against me. I said ok Frankie and I went to the state capital and filed bankruptcy. Ken accompanied me I wanted to keep him out of the financial mess I had gotten myself into. Frankie advised me on what I needed to do to file bankruptcy, and as a matter of fact he even had his attorney represent me on the day of the hearing. I felt as though a great burden had been taken off my shoulders, I had a combined outstanding debt of over fifty thousand dollars, how in the world had I gotten myself into this mess, and how was I going to get myself out of it. I felt that filing bankruptcy was my only option and I also knew that once I did that, I was at a greater risk of losing my home, but I still had the confidence that Frankie would be able to save my home.

Two years had passed, and I was still paying Frankie thirteen hundred dollars every month, I asked him what was the next move he informed me that I should start checking the local newspaper every day, because my home would soon be listed in the sheriff's sale. My heart was pounding from fear, but I kept hoping that the outcome would be in my favor. He told me that as soon as I saw the notice I should contact him right away. Ken and I kept looking in the newspaper then one day I saw the notice of sheriff sale for my home. I only hoped that none of my friends or co-workers saw the notice, since I lived in the same town as I worked everything was public knowledge. I informed Frankie that the sale had been posted in the paper, and he told me that I should go back to the state capital and file bankruptcy again. I asked him why, and he said that this will buy us more time. Reluctantly I did, I just followed his instructions I didn't know what else to do. This did delay the proceedings, and everything was put on hold. About ten months later, the notice for the sheriff's sale of my house reappeared in the newspaper again. I called Frankie to inform him that the notice had reappeared in the newspaper, but I kept getting taped messages with no return calls. I was beginning to worry a lot, because I sensed that something had gone terribly wrong.

Eventually I was able to reach someone who informed me that RRS had filed bankruptcy one month ago. I was devastated no one had made me aware of this I continued to make my payments until that time. I called Linda my cousin and told her what had happened she couldn't believe her ears, because she went through that same program earlier, and she was able to save her house. I had paid forty-two thousand dollars over the past three years to that company, and now they had just disappeared with my money. At first no one bought the house, it was not in the best of shape and they were asking too much money for it. It needed a new roof, siding, both front and back porches were a mess, the windows needed to be changed out. The sheriff's sale was held in Feb. 2001, I went to the sheriff's sale I'm not sure why I did that, I guess I was like a drowning man clutching at a straw. I had no money, I was about to lose the house I had worked so hard to get. We were still living in the house even after it went into foreclosure we didn't have to leave right away, so the money that I had been paying to RRS, I started saving. I was served notice that we had to vacate the premises, we were given two months in which to do so. Just before the end of the second month, I was advised to go to the sheriff's office and apply for a stay I did and was granted a few more months in the house.

I was very depressed I just barely did the things I needed to do. I tried to keep my distance from everyone including my own family I didn't want them to know that I was having such financial difficulties. I felt like a failure, I kept all of my emotions locked up inside, and I frequently cried when no one else was around. I also experienced a tremendous weight gain because all I did after work was eat and go to bed. I had gained fourteen pounds in one year I had gotten myself in one big mess.

Eventually I told my mother and Rebecca that we had to move. Rebecca had graduated college and was living back home she was becoming a very difficult person to live with. She felt that she could come and go as she pleased without saying anything to me. This created a lot of problems and we had a lot of heated arguments. I told them that I had lost the house, and that we had to move into an apartment. They were both disappointed and upset I informed them that they needed to start packing their things. We gave away and threw out lots of stuff, because we were moving from a house to an apartment we needed to de-clutter.

I received a letter from the sheriff's office stating that we had to vacate the premises within the next two weeks. That same night as we were all having dinner, the sheriff returned with a copy of the same letter and handed it to me he wanted to make sure that I received the letter. He told me that we had two weeks to leave, and that if we didn't find a place by then, the bank would put our things into storage and pay for the first month, and that we could stay in a hotel until we found a place. This was the ultimate I was so ashamed I could hardly face my family. This was when it really sank in that we had to move, none of us wanted to move.

Ken and I started apartment hunting we needed to get an apartment with three bedrooms. We looked at several apartments, but none of them met our criteria we were trying to compare apartments to the home we had just lost. Time was running out and we decided to go with a rental agency. Eventually we saw a listing for townhomes, within our price range. I wasn't very happy with the location, but when we checked it out we were pleasantly surprised. The development was only two years old and the town homes were located by the waterfront, on the outskirts of the city, with beautiful landscaping. It was also conveniently located minutes away from some of the major highways. We went into the rental office and took an application home. After looking over the application, it was evident that I couldn't put my name on the application, since one of their reasons for denial was bankruptcy.

We needed to get another person to cosign with Ken because one week's salary had to be equivalent to the rent, and his weekly salary didn't make it. The rent was one thousand three hundred and thirty five dollars each month. Once again I called Linda and told her our dilemma we needed another person to sign the application. She asked her daughter Kelly to sign the application with Ken, and that's how we were able to secure the apartment. We had until October 24th to vacate the premises, and we moved out on October 21st, that was cutting it really close. The apartment was spacious it had three bedrooms including a master bedroom, two and a half bathrooms, and a very large living dining area. My husband's friends came with a large truck and helped us move. Rebecca said that she wasn't moving with us, I told her that whatever she decided, we all had to be out of here before the 24th. She decided that she would move in with us temporarily. We settled into the apartment my mom had her bedroom and Rebecca had hers. It took a lot of getting used to, the complex was very noisy, there were lots of kids in the complex it was a very large place. I knew that I wouldn't want to stay there for a long time, but I knew that we had to get our finances together before we could ever think of moving again.

Ivy Joy Rose

It was a hot summer's day in July, and we had a very busy day at work as always. On returning home from work, my mom and I had dinner, we talked and everything seemed fine. I asked her how her day was, and she said everything was ok. After dinner I went out for a ride, while riding I realized how tired I was, so I decided to call it quits and go back home. I put my bike away, and flopped on the couch breathing very heavily thinking to myself once I got back into shape I'll never allow myself to get out of control again, because it took too much effort to lose weight.

Just then the phone rang, I answered it, and my sister-in-law Gladys was on the phone frantically telling me something was wrong with mom, she said she had just called her on her phone, and she was not making any sense. I ran upstairs to her room, and my mom was sitting in her rocking chair watching wheel of fortune, her favorite show. She smiled when she saw me, I asked her if she was ok and she said yes. I asked her if Gladys had called her, and she said yes, so I asked her why she didn't speak with her, and she said I don't know. This response seemed somewhat strange, so I decided to switch the conversation and ask her questions that would require more than just a yes or no answer. She looked at me for a few seconds, she was thinking about the answer, it was not automatic as it should have been, and when she answered, her speech was slow and somewhat slurred.

I quickly checked her blood sugar, my mom was a diabetic. Her blood sugar was over two hundred she had just finished dinner and eaten a mango. I grabbed her blood pressure kit, and made several attempts to take her BP, but it kept reading error. I called 911 and told them my mom was having a stroke. Of course they wanted to know what were her signs and symptoms, I told them about the slurred speech and her obvious confusion. They were on their way. My sister in law kept calling me every few seconds asking if the squad had gotten there as yet, and telling me they were on their way also. I was so nervous by this time I kept running down stairs to check for the squad, and running back up to check on my mom. It seemed an eternity before they arrived when they did I showed them to my mom's room.

They greeted her, and asked her a few questions which she answered appropriately. The EMT did a few routine neurological checks and he told me he didn't believe she was having a stroke because her answers were appropriate. I asked him to take her pressure since I could not get a reading on her BP machine, when he did her pressure was 264/140. They asked for a list of her medications, and I gave it to them. The EMT then told my mom they were going to take her to the hospital for treatment because her pressure was too high. I rode in the squad with my mom, and requested that they take her to the hospital of my choice but they refused, which I already knew they would.

We had just moved to this town, and I had little knowledge of the reputation of this hospital. I didn't know any of the doctors who practiced there either. When we arrived at the ER, they immediately began working her up, drawing blood starting IV's and giving her medication to help lower her BP. The ER doctor was still questioning whether or not she was having a stroke, because she was still awake alert and oriented, and answering their questions appropriately. To them she seemed ok, but my family and I knew she was not her normal self. Adrian and Gladys arrived, and as we waited at her bedside in the ER, I saw a familiar face come through the doors it was one of the doctors I worked with at another hospital. I went over to him and told him my mom was just brought into the ER, and that we thought she was having a stroke. I told him that I did not know any doctor's there and I was very concerned about the care she would receive. He was very sympathetic and offered to accept her case. He said he would be her admitting doctor, and he would call in the best specialists for her specific needs. I felt a great sense of relief he was someone I knew I could trust to do his best for my mom. I was very grateful and thankful all at the same time.

He did a neurological exam on my mom, and he too was not completely sure she was having a stroke he said there was a very fine line whether or not she was having a stroke. He felt somehow she was fooling him. He ordered a ct. scan of the head "stat," a neurological consult and neurological checks every hour. He wrote an order for her to be transferred to a telemetry floor so she could be closely monitored. She was taken to the X-Ray dept. around 11p.m. for the ct. scan of the head. She was in the X-Ray dept. for half an hour, and when she returned we helped her back to bed, she was still alert and knew what was happening. It was around the change of shift, and the nurse who was taking care of her, told us there were no telemetry beds available, but they would put her in a different area in the ER, where she would be monitored throughout the night, until she could be transferred to telemetry.

Her blood pressure improved from the medication she received, we made her comfortable, Ken and Rebecca also arrived at the ER we were all concerned about her situation. It was after midnight when we decided we would all go home, so she could have a restful night. Rebecca informed me she felt that it was my husband's fault my mom had the stroke. I asked her why she felt this way, and she said about two to three weeks ago her grandmother had a scare. She said your husband was moving in some furniture and he left the door ajar while he went to get the rest of the furniture. My mom got scared when she saw the door open, and no one answered when she called. She said she got butterflies in her stomach. Soon after my husband returned with the furniture and they all laughed over the incident. I told her whatever happened was unintentional and no harm was intended, and if that was the case my mom would have had a stroke right then, not two or three weeks later. She said there you go again taking his side. This was no time to get into an argument with her, I said good night and went off to bed, I wanted to get some sleep so I could get up early the next morning and stop by to see my mom before going off to work. I couldn't fall asleep, I stayed awake most of the night I was worried about my mom, and I also worried about my daughter, I had a feeling she wanted to create some problems with my husband, whom she admittedly never liked.

The next morning I got out of bed at five-thirty A.M. showered got dressed for work then I called the ER to get an update on my mother's condition. I spoke with the nurse who took care of her during the night, and she told me my mom had an uneventful night, she was ok and she was just transferred to the telemetry unit. She transferred my call to the nurse who would be taking care of my mother. I asked the nurse who had just received my mom from the ER how she was doing, she said she was ok, but then she asked me if my mom does not speak much, because she was not answering her questions. I told her my mom loves to chat something didn't seem right. I went straight to the hospital to my mother's room. It was about 6:15 A.M. around the change of shift again. When I walked into the room my mom appeared to be asleep. I called her name softly a few times, and when she opened her eyes she was looking away from where I was standing, I immediately knew something had gone wrong. I thought maybe she was a bit disoriented because of the unfamiliar surroundings, but I soon realized she was responding to my voice but she couldn't speak, I then realized she had right sided paralysis she could not move her right arm or right leg, my mother had a stroke in the middle of the night sometime between midnight and six A.M. and no one recognized it. It wasn't until I arrived at 6:15 A.M. in the morning and found the changes in her condition. I went to the nurse's station and asked for the nurse, I took her to my mom's bedside and told her my mother's condition had deteriorated sometime during the night, and no one ever noticed. She told me she had just received my mom from the ER, and she would make the doctor aware.

I decided I would wait for the neurologist to arrive before going to work I called my manager and told her my mom had a stroke and I would be late coming in. I knew it would have been a very busy day at work, but at this point I couldn't leave my mother's bedside. I asked the nurse to call the neurologist and inform her that my mom's condition had deteriorated during the night. I kept checking with the nurse, and she kept telling me she had made several calls to the doctor which she had not returned. I called my job, and informed them I wouldn't make it into work because I was waiting for the doctor to arrive. After a few hours of going back and forth to the nurse's station without any response from the neurologist, I asked the nurse to call the admitting doctor and have him recommend a different doctor for my mom. I also requested to speak to the nursing supervisor. Several hours had already passed imagine a new stroke victim lying in the hospital bed from the night before without appropriate treatment.

The supervisor became involved, she started making calls herself and she was able to get things moving. The neurologist arrived at approximately two pm. She claimed the information she received about my mom was not indicative of a stroke. My mom was immediately started on heparin therapy. Her admitting doctor showed me where he ordered neurological checks to be done every hour throughout the night, they were checked off as done, but obviously someone missed important signs and symptoms, because some time during the night, my mom had a stroke and no one had noticed, it wasn't until I arrived in the morning and made them aware something had gone terribly wrong. We all stayed there very late into the night, just to make sure her treatments were implemented in a timely manner before going home. I showered and went to bed, but I tried to stay awake until Rebecca came in, it was Thursday and that was her late day getting in from school, she was finishing up her internship program in interior design.

The Midnight Brawl

Just as I was about to fall asleep, I heard Rebecca speaking loudly downstairs and she seemed to be upset. I got out of bed and went downstairs to find out what the problem was. She was eating and watching TV, she said your man is moving things around, he moved something I left on the plant stand, and he's doing that because he is vindictive. She kept using profanity I told her I was going back to bed because I was tired, and when she felt like talking in a rational manner I would be more than willing to listen to her and I went back to bed. Shortly after, the TV was blasting I asked her to turn it down and she did. I heard her go to her room and closed the door behind her. I was finally going to get some sleep.

As I started to doze off, I heard clapping and the familiar sounds of my exercise tape playing very loud. Rebecca was trying my patience which I was very short of because I was so tired. I did not move I stayed in bed only hoping she would stop. I hoped the noise wouldn't disturb Ken, since he got up at four-thirty every morning to go to work. By now it was after midnight and very obvious Rebecca wanted to start something. Suddenly Ken jumped out of bed, he opened the door and stood at the top of the stairs and yelled to Rebecca to tone it down. He said I'm trying to get some sleep I have to get up early in the morning.

This is the opening she was waiting for she started cursing and yelling very loud, and for some unknown reason I decided I would remain in bed and allow them to settle their battle. This was a bad decision. I heard Rebecca at the top of the stairs they were both very loud and yelling at each other I still did not get up, then I heard him saying get out of my face, and I heard her saying you pushed me. That was enough I jumped out of bed, Ken was still standing at the top of the stairs and Rebecca was in the living room still cursing and heading towards the entertainment center. Suddenly there was a big bang we both ran down the stairs, Rebecca had pulled Ken's stereo and speaker off the shelf and thrown them on the floor. She was furious they were both cursing and going towards each other everything was moving very fast I got in the middle trying to keep both of them away from each other, I had both of my arms outstretched one arm toward each of them, I was begging both of them to stop, but neither one of them was listening to me. I was literally trapped in the middle. I had an intense feeling of fear and helplessness, everything was happening very fast, I lost my balance and the next thing I knew Rebecca had jumped on Ken's back and she was throwing punches at him, she is five feet two inches tall and he is six feet two inches tall. He was saying get off of me I noticed that he had the phone in his hand. I heard Rebecca saying you hit me look at this, I have a lump on my forehead.

Rebecca had a friend who lived in the same complex as we did. She went over there and called the cops. When they arrived they spoke with her, then they came to our apartment to speak with both Ken and I. The cop advised Rebecca to start planning on finding her own place, since it was obvious she didn't get along with Ken. She came back home, went to her room and stayed there for the rest of the night. It was almost three a.m. I went to bed and spoke with Ken, I told him after he asked Rebecca to tone it down he should have come back into the room and closed the door, and she would not have anyone to argue with. It was almost time to get up and get ready for work, I got no sleep, but I couldn't stay out of work another day.

I visited my mom to make sure that she was ok before going to work. They were making arrangements to transfer her to the stroke unit. I stayed with her until the transfer was done, then I went on to work all the time wondering how I was going to function that day. After I completed my shift, I went straight back to the hospital to visit my mom. I stayed a little while then went home. I needed to get some sleep.

Rebecca was there when I arrived, she had left work early she said that her supervisor saw the lump on her forehead and sent her home early. Rebecca said that she did not get any sleep the night before. We talked about the incident I told her that it was very apparent that she was looking to start a fight because she kept picking on every little thing. I also reminded her that it was unfair and disrespectful to both Ken and I to be making noise in the middle of the night, and it was wrong to get into his face, because anytime you step into someone else's space, you should be prepared, because you never know how that person will react. I told Rebecca that I was ashamed and humiliated over the entire situation that it was ghetto behavior, and in all of my life I had never been involved in anything like that. I reminded her that she had a very good upbringing, and it was very difficult for me to comprehend this. Rebecca still didn't think that she had done anything wrong in this entire situation.

Ken arrived home and started fussing over his broken stereo, he said that he wanted it fixed by Friday, and that if it wasn't fixed that other things would be broken. Rebecca heard him and came out of her room they started arguing again, it was escalating she picked up a shoe, and that's when I informed them both that I was leaving, I had enough. I took Rebecca into her room and closed the door, she picked up the phone and called the cops and told them there had been an altercation, I took the phone from her, and told the cops that they were arguing, but there was no altercation. Two cops showed up, one of them took Rebecca into the living room and the other cop took Ken into the kitchen. They spoke with both of them and told each of them not to say anything to each other, but should go through me if either one had anything to say to the other. That night we all turned into bed, but I'm still not sure if anyone ever slept that night.

The following day I went to the hospital, I had started a routine I'd go there and give my mom a bath before going to work. I wanted to make sure that she was being taken care of. She was scheduled for a few x-ray procedures that day, and they came to take her to the x-ray dept. I made her bed and left for work. My work day was uneventful I was very quiet, didn't say much to any of my co-workers, they knew that my mom was very sick, so everyone just assumed that I was preoccupied with my mother's condition. After work I returned to the hospital my mom was just returning from one of her x-ray procedures. I helped her back to bed, and immediately noticed that her right arm was significantly swollen from the elbow down to the hand. I showed it to her nurse, and asked her what happened, she had no idea. She called the x-ray department since she was there most of the day, and no one could give an account of why her arm was swollen. The doctor was notified and when he visited, he told me that he felt that my mom had developed a deep vein thrombosis in her right arm, and that she was already on heparin which was the treatment of choice for that condition.

Mentally my mom was making some progress, she was getting out of bed with assistance and she was eating a little, things were looking up but the swelling in her right arm was getting worse. She was once again transferred out of the stroke unit into a regular medical floor her bed was just outside the nurse's station. The swelling in my mother's arm continued to get worse, it had moved up above her elbow to her shoulders, her finger tips were purple the entire arm was ecchymotic and painful to touch. I asked to speak with the supervisor and when she came I took her to my mom's room and showed her the condition of my mother's right arm. I told her that I was fed up with the poor treatment my mother had been receiving ever since she was hospitalized there and that I wanted to have all of her doctors called and that they needed to figure out what was really happening.

The nursing supervisor got things moving again, it was discovered that my mom did not have a DVT in that arm, but someone had tried to start an intravenous in that arm the day she had all of those x-ray procedures scheduled, and she had been bleeding in that arm since that time. She had lost so much blood, that she had to be transfused with two units of packed red blood cells. The doctor told me that he would have to stop the heparin, since that's a blood thinner. He also said that it's been one week since your mom has been on heparin and there were no signs of a recurrent stroke, so he felt that it was safe to take her off. The treatment for the arm was elevation and warm soaks, the nurse told me that she would order the equipment. I elevated my mom's arm on a pillow, made her comfortable and went home. The next morning I went to visit my mom she still had not received any treatment on her arm. I went to her nurse and said that it has been almost twenty four hours since the doctor ordered warm soaks for my mom's arm I was here when he ordered it, and it still has not been applied. I said I really don't want to be bitchy, but if it's not started soon I will explode. She apologized and got it started soon after.

Her condition started to worsen again her liver functions were elevated and the doctor told me that she may be going into renal failure, he thought that it could be due to the breakdown of the blood cells which had pooled in her muscles in her arm. He called in a kidney specialist. Luckily that was not the case the infection control specialist realized that she was not emptying her bladder completely and that was causing a back flow of urine into her kidneys. The problem was resolved by inserting a Foley catheter to insure complete drainage. Her mental status had taken a dip also, she was not responding like she had been earlier. I brought this to the doctor's attention, after examining her he agreed with me, he said Adrianna you're very observant, you can always pick up changes with your mom. He ordered a repeat ct. scan of the head, she had been off heparin for three days, and none of the doctors thought of putting her on an oral anticoagulant. The results of the ct. scan showed she had a recurrent stroke which was more extensive than the previous one.

Once again they had screwed up she was put on an oral anticoagulant. Her general condition had deteriorated she was not eating anything at all. It was always difficult to draw blood from her veins, so they decided to insert a PICC line, this allowed easy access to blood draw and intravenous fluids. She also had to have a feeding tube inserted for nutritional purposes, since she couldn't eat. They had started physical therapy on her, but all of this had to be put on hold. Both family and friends visited frequently I assumed they thought she wouldn't make it out of the hospital alive, but I always had the feeling she would make it out of there.

My sister in law Gladys and my cousin Dari took turns caring for her, one of us was always there making sure she was repositioned every couple of hours, and we even got her out of bed to the chair. This kept her from having skin break down and developing bed sores. Most importantly we kept talking to her as though everything was ok. My mom was eighty two years old at the time she was the oldest one in the family. Prior to the stroke she was totally independent she did everything for herself, and she took walks every day, the only thing she didn't do was drive. She read the newspaper daily, watched CNN, Court TV, Judge Judy, Wheel of Fortune and Jeopardy those were her favorite shows. She also enjoyed sports and current events. I didn't have to watch the news or read the newspaper, she kept me informed. I always teased her and told her that she should apply for a job as a news anchor.

One day when I got home from the hospital, Rebecca was there with her cousin Nina. They were packing her clothes into suitcases, I asked what she was doing, and she said that she was leaving, I tried to talk her out of it, but she didn't listen actually she was hardly speaking to me. They brought her suitcases down and packed them into the car then they came back into the house. Nina asked about the incident, and I told her what happened. She asked to speak with Ken.

After they were done talking, Rebecca said I can't believe that you were speaking to him in such a friendly manner. Nina said how did you expect me to speak to him, and Rebecca said I wanted you to kick his ass. Nina said girl you need to have some respect for your mother and step-father, I know you told me that you don't like him, but even if you don't like him you should at least show respect. She said just take a look around at your environment, you have everything and most girls your age, would give anything just to have one fourth of what you have, and you don't appreciate any of it. She said you have a beautiful room with everything in it you have a car which your mom is paying for, including the insurance, you get your meals cooked, and you don't help to do anything around the house, and you are the one who started this mess in the first place, so what do you expect me to say.

Nina said you know what's wrong, is that you are a selfish spoilt brat. She said my cousin you are beautiful on the outside, but on the inside you are selfish and rotten. You need to change your ways, because if you don't and you continue to think that you can get up into people's faces, these "n . . . ."s out here will fuck you up. Rebecca was stunned, you should have seen the look of disbelief on her face, she had actually brought Nina to fight Ken she couldn't believe that Nina actually turned against her. Nina told her that she should apologize to both of us, but of course she didn't. Nina told me that she was taking Rebecca to their aunt's house where she would be staying.

The following day I received several phone calls telling me that Rebecca had sent out e-mails to everyone on her mailing list, which stated that Ken had assaulted her and that her mother just stood there and watched and didn't try to stop it, so she needed their help. My response was please this is just a little too much for me to handle. My mom is gravely ill and I need to put all of my energy into her care. The following day Rebecca came back for more of her belongings this went without incident. The next day two cops came to the apartment and served Ken a subpoena to appear in court on assault charges. The court date was set for August 2nd. The very next day she arrived with a cop to get some more of her clothes, I asked her why she brought the cop she said that she needed protection from my husband. I said since when do you need protection from him she said you stood there and didn't do anything when he punched me. I reminded her that she was the one who started it, with the noise, then cursing and getting up in his face, and when the situation got out of control that I was literally trapped in the middle, trying to keep them apart. I asked her to please stop bringing the cops here because it was embarrassing. Her response was every-time I need to get something I will bring the cops with me, that's when I told her that I would change my locks on the door, and that she would have to make arrangements with me without the cops to get the remainder of her belongings. Two days later the cops arrived again, this time they brought restraining orders against Ken. This court date was set for August 3rd.

This was turning into a nightmare I wondered what would be next. One Saturday morning Ken went downstairs to get the newspaper, and to his surprise someone had smashed in the right side back window of the jeep. It appeared as though someone had taken a baseball bat to the window. We called the cops and later made out a police report. Estimates for replacement ranged from five hundred dollars and up our deductible was five hundred dollars that meant we had to foot the bill. Ken covered the opening with tape and plastic and we drove around like that for a few weeks until we could have it fixed.

Ken had started school he was learning to drive tractor trailers. This had been a dream of his for a very long time. Every day after work, he dropped me off at the hospital on his way to school, then after school he visited my mom. One evening Rebecca came to visit her grandmother I was on the phone with Ken, shortly after she left, only to return a few minutes later. She said she was going to the nurse's station to make a phone call. Apparently she asked to see the charge nurse then she asked her how well she knew me the nurse told her she only knew me from visiting my mom every day. Rebecca pulled out a copy of the restraining order from her hand bag, gave it to the nurse and told her if Ken ever visited her grandmother again, they should call the cops. She then took a copy to the information desk in the main lobby and left it there instructing them to do the same. The nurse came into the room with the restraining order and asked me what was going on and who Rebecca was. I told her she is my daughter and she and my husband were having some serious issues, and she put a restraining order against him coming to see my mom. The nurse put her arms around me, and said I'm so sorry you are going through this while your mom is so ill. You are here every morning and evening providing such good care and support to your mom, and this is the first time I have seen her. Instead of her offering you support, this is what she's doing to you. I was so embarrassed she was bringing our problems at home into the hospital where it did not belong. The nurse said if she's so concerned how come she's never there to help care for her grandmother.

That night the phone rang in my mother's room, when I answered it was Ken saying I'll be in the jeep waiting for you. I detected something was wrong. I told him I was giving my mom a bath, and he should come up as usual. He said he was on his way up and when he stopped at the desk to get a pass to come up, they asked his name, and when he told them the guards told him there was a restraining order against him and they escorted him out of the hospital. He said he was very embarrassed. I tried to keep my cool, I did not want my mother to know about any of this mess that was happening, Ken and my mom got along very well, they liked each other. After giving my mom her bath, I made her comfortable and kissed her goodnight. I went to the desk at the main lobby, and spoke with the guards I told them my mom had been hospitalized there for three weeks, she couldn't speak and she definitely did not put a restraining order against Ken. I couldn't understand how this was happening they apologized and allowed him to come back in to see my mom even though visiting hours were over by then. After we left we went straight to the precinct and reported this matter. We were told nothing could be done because the order was already in, but we could go to court to get it removed, or wait until the court hearing. We decided to wait for the hearing which was only a few days away.

Ken retained an attorney his fee was three thousand five hundred to represent him in both cases. On August second we went to court, Rebecca did not show up. The judge postponed the case for a different date, but the attorney had a prior commitment for that date. Ken and I were on our way to the hospital he was going to drop me off there and continue onto school. We were running a little late, and he caught the end of the yellow light. Out of nowhere we saw the flashing lights and we were pulled over. The cop asked us where we were going, we told him to the hospital to visit my mom. He asked to see Ken's license, insurance and registration. We produced them, but the registration had expired. I kept looking for the current registration card, but couldn't find it. The cop went back to his car and was there for a while, two other cop cars arrived, and when the cop returned he asked Ken for his keys and told us to step out of the car. I said why are you asking us to get out of the car? He said your registration has expired and I'm having your jeep impounded. I pleaded with him not to have our truck towed away, and promised I would have it taken care of the following day. I was dealing with so many stressful issues I had completely overlooked the registration renewal. He said he couldn't, the tow truck arrived and towed the jeep away. I was overwhelmed I started crying I thought what the hell could be next. We were just a few blocks from the hospital, it must have been about 100 degrees it was in the middle of July, and that fat pig had no mercy on us. I never speak badly of cops, but this one made me real angry. We walked to the hospital, and Ken took a cab back home. He couldn't visit my mom because the restraining order was still in place and we hadn't gone to court as yet to have it removed. Adrian was visiting that night he took me home after visiting was over.

The Hearing

The following day was the hearing for Rebecca's charges against Ken. Ken drove his work van to court, our car was impounded the day before, and we had no time to address that issue. We arrived at the court and waited for the attorney who arrived about fifteen minutes later. Rebecca arrived about half an hour late, but their case had not been called as yet. She kept pacing back and forth, and looking as though she was mad as hell. She called me on the phone a few times and spoke with me, even crying at times. I got up and hugged her. Throughout all of this I felt very sorry for her, even though she has done some hurt full things she is still my only child and I love her dearly. I guess this is unconditional love.

Their case was eventually called, and the cop informed me that I had to remain outside of the courtroom, because both Rebecca and Ken had listed me as their witness, and I couldn't go into the room until I was called. It seemed like an eternity as I nervously waited. I wanted to run away, why did I have to be in this situation? Once again I was caught in the middle. Eventually I was called to the witness stand, where I took the oath. The lawyer told me to tell the court the events of the night of July ninth. I took a deep breath, and told him exactly what happened that night. I told him that I did not see everything, not in the beginning because at first I didn't get out of my bed. I told him what I heard and what I saw and that everything was happening so fast, it was almost impossible to rehash everything perfectly, but I would do my best to tell the truth. At the end of my testimony, the Judge asked me if Rebecca had a lump on her forehead and I said yes she did.

The lawyer asked me if my husband had ever been verbally abusive to my daughter, I said no, and I added that's not to say they haven't had disagreements and arguments like any other family, but if anyone had been verbally abusive, it was my daughter to both my husband and I. I said for example, when things aren't going her way she'll not hesitate to curse you out. Then I gave him another example of the time when Ken was teaching Rebecca to drive, and she got mad at him because he told her she needed to pay attention to where she was going and learn her way around, because she wouldn't have him or me with her all of the time. When they got home, she cursed him out beyond belief. Ken called me at work, and told me he was leaving, because he couldn't take it anymore. When I got home I told Rebecca I wanted to speak to her, she went upstairs to her room slammed the door and refused to speak to me. I told him that was only one example of many instances towards either one of us. Those were the only questions I was asked then I was told to leave the courtroom. I waited for almost an hour before the lawyer came out of the courtroom. He told me the judge had thrown out all of the charges with the exception he was leaving the restraining order against him from going to her place of business or residence. When Ken came out of the court room he cried, and that was the first time I saw my husband cry.

After leaving there, we went directly to the motor vehicle to renew the registration to our jeep. The place was packed we waited for almost two hours before we were able to get our vehicle registered. With registration in hand, we headed back home to the precinct to pick up the report which no one could find. We sat there for an eternity waiting for fat pig to show up with the report. We asked them where our jeep was, and they told us it had been towed two towns away, it was already late in the day and by the time we arrived the place was closed. This meant we had to pay an additional day of storage fee. After all of the running around, Ken and I visited my mom. It was very late and visiting hours were over, but the staff always allowed us to visit no matter what time we arrived. We had to remain strong for my mom and not letting her know any of what was happening between Rebecca and us. My mom was better now and she was scheduled to be transferred from the hospital to the rehab the following day. My brother Adrian and his wife Gladys offered to accompany my mom to the rehab, since Ken and I had to attend his nephew's wedding.

The following day we picked up the jeep, I didn't want to go to the wedding, but we had already sent in our response and Ken had agreed to be the MC. It was just a terrible time for us, with my mom's illness and Rebecca's madness I didn't want to be around anyone. I consider myself to be a very generous person, but we were so broke at this point, we couldn't afford to give the bride and groom a gift. I was embarrassed about this. I couldn't even afford to get my hair done I wore a wig which I kept for emergencies. I was miserable, I couldn't have fun I just wanted to get out of there.

The following day was August 4th, my birthday. We visited my mom in the rehab, Rebecca had already visited and left me a card and gift at my mom's bedside when I opened the gift it was a musical ceramic angel. I later called and thanked her for the gift. Ken and I went out to dinner for my birthday after we left the rehab center. This new place was further away from where I lived, so I only visited my mom after work every day, I couldn't go there before work. My mom had a very good roommate, she was a younger woman who looked out for my mom and called for help whenever she thought my mom needed help because she still couldn't speak. I appreciated that very much.

Slowly but surely my mom's condition started to improve, she still wasn't eating, she was fed through her gastric feeding tube. The speech pathologist called me up one day while I was at work she told me she wanted to schedule my mom for a swallowing test to see if she was able to swallow, I told her it was ok. I met my mom at the hospital and stayed with her until the test was completed. The test showed my mom was able to swallow and the very next day she was put on a pureed diet. She wouldn't eat, we tried everything, we tried feeding her but she refused, the only thing she ate off the tray was the crackers.

Ken and I went to visit my mom after church one Sunday. As we signed in I noticed that Rebecca and her aunt had just signed in about ten minutes before us. I told Ken she was there and he decided he would sit in the lobby and not come in with me. I greeted both of them and we talked for a while. They left after half an hour or so and Ken came into my mom's room where we stayed until visiting hours were over. On the way home my phone rang, I saw Rebecca's name and my heart sank, I knew it wasn't going to be a friendly call. She said I don't appreciate what you did to me today, I asked her what did I do, and she said you know fully well what you did you brought that man there even though you knew I was there. I said that was the reason why he didn't come into the room when we saw your name on the guest list he decided to stay away, and anyway I had no clue when you would visit your grandmother. She said if that's the way you want it that's fine because the next time I visit my granny, I'll bring Monroe with me, that's her biological dad whom she hasn't seen in a very long time. I said go ahead and bring him am I supposed to be afraid of him she said fine and hung up the phone. The most hurtful part about this conversation was the fact that Monroe has never supported her, he has never paid child support, not one cent, she rarely spoke with him, and all of a sudden she was using him as a threat to me. She tried calling me back, but I refused to answer my phone. I told Ken what she said about bringing her father with her to the rehab and his answer was the same as mine he said so what, am I supposed to be afraid of him.

After we got home that night, I showered and went to bed Ken was on the computer and the doorbell rang, it must have been after 10pm. He went down to answer the door, I looked out the window and saw the flashing lights from two cop cars, and Rebecca's car I ran downstairs and Ken was standing at the door Rebecca wanted to get in but Ken did not allow her to. I said why are you here with the cops? This was her seventh trip here with them. The cop said that she came to get her things. I told him that we had already made arrangements for her to get her belongings and she was just doing this out of spite. She was pissed off because Ken visited her grandmother while she was there. I was so angry I went upstairs and gathered whatever she had left in her room and took it to her. I told her that she was never to come back here with the cops again, and that if she ever did that I as her mother and she being my only child, that I would put restraining orders against her coming to my apartment.

After she left, I was so angry I called her aunt and told her what she had done. I asked her to please speak with Rebecca because if she ever did that again, I would file a restraining order against her for harassment. Her aunt could not believe that Rebecca had driven all the way over there that night to get things which she didn't need to have at that time. She promised me that she would speak to her when she came back. The already strained relationship between Rebecca and I had just become worse. This was the turning point for me, I decided that I would not have anything to do with Rebecca until she came to her senses, I was fed up it was taking too much out of me I still had the stress of my sick mother to deal with.

Rebecca still wasn't done we received another summons from the domestic court stating that Ken had violated the restraining order by visiting my mom at the rehab while she was there, and that the plaintiff's wife (that's me, who's her mother) was speaking to her on Ken's behalf and she wanted this stopped. We couldn't believe this, it seemed like a nightmare. On the day of the trial we arrived in court this time without an attorney because we couldn't afford one. The judge read her complaints then he asked her to present her case which was frivolous. He listened to her then he said motion denied I would like all of you to get out of my court room in a very angry tone. I tried to ask him how I could prevent her from coming to the house with the cops, but he didn't want to hear anything. Ken told the judge that she kept coming to the house the judge asked her if she wanted to drop the restraining charges and she said no. Then he yelled at her and said why are you going to his house are you trying to antagonize him, do not go back there, and with that he told us all to leave.

On the way home I started to cry, I was so embarrassed that the judge had actually thrown us out of the court room, it was the same judge who had presided over the first case. Ken and I started arguing over silly things, I guess we were both frustrated. We went to visit my mom, and as we pulled up in the parking lot Rebecca's car was there. Ken did not stay he told me to call him when I was ready to leave. I was teary eyed when I went in to see my mom. Rebecca came over to me and said don't let him boss you around or don't allow him to say bad things about me to you. It was as if she didn't have anything to do with this entire situation. I just looked at her and said that I was upset and tired over the entire situation and I wanted this nightmare to be over. I told her that I was done and if they ever had to appear in court again that I would not be present, I refuse to be a part of this any longer. Rebecca called everyone and told them that she won the case, to that I said whatever. I spent the rest of the day with my mom her condition was improving on a daily basis.

One day on my way to the rehab, I stopped at a fast food place and ordered fried chicken and French fries for my dinner. I took it with me so that I could have dinner with my mom. It was a beautiful summer's afternoon the weather was good, I put my mom in a wheelchair and took her outside. We sat in the gazebo Rebecca and my niece Kenya were also visiting, we were all sitting there I offered them some of my dinner, Kenya said she had a dinner engagement and she would be leaving soon, Rebecca took some of the chicken. I offered some to my mom, but she shook her head and gestured no. I kept offering it to her and eventually she agreed to have some. I broke a very small piece of the breast and gave it to her when she tasted it she made a funny face as though it was horrible. My mom hadn't eaten anything for over one month. I said to her remember you used to like fried chicken she looked at me, I said try another piece and she did I kept giving her more and she kept eating it. I kept telling her to chew it slowly and thoroughly because I didn't want her to choke on it. She ate a whole piece of chicken, I was so happy. The following day I called the speech pathologist and told her that my mom had eaten fried chicken, she was alarmed and concerned, I asked her to change her diet from pureed to mechanical soft, because I realized that the reason she wasn't eating was because she didn't like the pureed food. As soon as they changed her diet, my mom started eating again.

The entire team at the rehab did a wonderful job with my mom. When she arrived there on august 3rd, she was lying flat on her back and not able to do anything for herself. I had reservations when my mom first arrived at the rehab center, I didn't think that they could have done much for her, but just after one month and twenty days my mom was up walking with a cane, she was feeding herself she was climbing stairs, and she was able to go to the bathroom on her own.

She was discharged from the rehab on September 23rd. Ken and I took my mom home in the jeep she was able to get into the jeep with some help. I took the week off when my mom came home since this was going to be a big adjustment. In the mean time I had every one I knew trying to help me find someone to take care of my mom while I was at work. We were very lucky to find a very nice woman from my home town, her name was Desiree. She was new to the US and looking for a job. We hit it off right away she was very good to my mom. My vacation was up and I returned to work feeling very good that I had found a good person to care for my mom. Two and a half weeks later she received a call that her husband was very ill and he was hospitalized. Her family was telling her that she should go back home to be with him. She was crying and asked me what she should do. I told her that as much as I would like her to stay and care for my mom I think that she should go home to her husband, because if anything happened she would never be able to forgive herself. She said that she felt badly leaving Ivy and she wondered what I was going to do. I told her not to worry, that I would have to figure something out. I was worried I didn't know what I would do, or who I would find at such short notice, I had to take more time off. I asked everyone I knew to help me to find someone. Her last day was on Friday, and by Sunday the phone calls were coming in with people who were interested in the job.

I interviewed three people and chose Della. This was a difficult task I never had to do anything like this before, and I felt badly for the two people who didn't get the job. Della told me that she had eighteen kids I said oh you mean eight she said no I made eighteen kids and three of them died, so now I have fifteen. I said lady you must have a few loose screws and she laughed. Della was ok but she was not as good as Desiree. I was considering getting my mom into a medical day care center, but their hours of operation was not compatible with my working hours. My mom had an occupational therapist, a speech therapist, and a physical therapist that came to the house to help her regain her strength and independence. Ironically the physical therapist's wife is a very good friend of mine her name is Kate and my mom knew them so she felt very comfortable with him.

I frequently felt all alone in this whole wide world with all of my problems. I often thought that Ken was not supportive enough. I didn't think that he completely understood the extent of my problems, both emotional and financial. I took care of my mother on the weekends, since I couldn't afford to pay for weekend help also. Her social security benefit was approximately six hundred dollars monthly, and that only covered one half of the cost of her caretaker. The other half came from my salary. That placed a financial strain on my budget, but there were no other choices for me. My social life was abruptly put on hold. I couldn't go out on the weekends anymore I stayed at home and took care of my mom. Ken started going out without me, this started many arguments between us. We decided that we would all go over to the city for a getaway weekend. The plan included taking my mom with us so that she would also have a change of scenery herself. Arrangements were made to stay with my mom's God sister Olga and her family in Brooklyn, which would allow us the opportunity to go out and have some fun.

We drove over to the city after work on Friday and every one was very happy to see how well my mom was doing. We had planned to go out both on Friday and Saturday nights. It was getting to be very late, and I noticed that Ken was not making any effort to go out so I decided that I would go to bed. I said what the hell, tomorrow is another day, and we had plans to attend a dinner and dance on Saturday night. Ken came to bed, but he appeared to be very restless. He complained about being hungry, even though we had already eaten dinner. Then he started complaining about how hot he was and that he couldn't sleep. I suggested that he should just sleep in his underwear, but that seemed to annoy him. He got out of bed and went into the living room, sitting there by himself.

My cousin Dawn came home from work around midnight, and I heard them talking. Soon after Ken came back into the bedroom and sat on the bed for a few minutes, then he got up and left again. At this point I was beginning to become suspicious of his behavior. I got up and went into the living room, by then Ken had changed his clothes, and was heading for the door. I asked him where he was going, but he didn't answer. I followed him to the door and called him a no good mother fucker, I also told him that this marriage was over. He left anyway without responding. I was extremely angry. When I woke up the following day, I noticed that he was sleeping on the couch in the living room. He said good morning Adrianna but I wasn't going to speak to him, so I didn't respond. After breakfast, I left for my hair appointment he offered to take me to my appointment, but I refused his offer and walked there. That night we didn't go anywhere either, so much for a fun weekend in the city.

The following day I went to Manhattan to the garment district. I went on a shopping spree to my favorite store, within twenty minutes I had spent six-hundred dollars. That made me feel good, shopping always relieves tension. My cousin Dawn had accompanied me shopping, and after my spree was over we took the subway back to Brooklyn where she lived. As we were preparing to leave, Ken put on a new black kangol he bought and looked over my way just to make sure that I had seen it I said to myself big deal I bought over six hundred dollars of clothes today, now you beat that. All the way home I reflected on the fact that we were supposed to have a fun weekend in the city, but instead it turned out to be horrible. It wasn't all bad, because my mom had a weekend out of the house this was a good change for her, and she was able to see some of her friends. I felt all alone in the whole wide world, my entire life was in turmoil and I didn't know who to turn to. The one thing that kept me going was the fact that I had to stay strong for my mother, she needed me and I just couldn't disappoint her, and every time I looked at her she smiled at me as to say everything is going to be all right. Linda came to my rescue she agreed to take care of my mom one weekend every month, so that I could have some me time. She traveled all the way from Long Island to NJ to help take care of her aunt.

Ken made a trip to Virginia, it was work related after he delivered his freight he called and said that he was too tired to drive back home that night. That was atypical of Ken, he always wanted to turn right around and come back home, but I agreed with him saying that if you're tired the smart thing to do is to get some sleep before driving back home. He said that he was hungry he'd get something to eat then find a hotel for the night. My mom and I were having dinner when Ken arrived home the following evening he appeared to be in an awfully good mood, this seemed very strange to me, because whenever he returned from a long trip, he was always tired and irritable. He was wearing a grey hoodie when he came in, the apartment was warm he went upstairs and changed into a tee-shirt. When he came back down he said something to me, and as I turned around to look at him, my heart sank. Ken had the biggest hickey on the left side of his neck that I'd ever seen. My blood pressure hit the ceiling, I felt my veins pounding I quickly tried to regain my composure, because I didn't want to create a scene in front of my mother. I didn't want to upset her and cause her blood pressure to go up under any circumstance. My mom ate very slowly I couldn't wait for her to finish her dinner, as soon as she was done I took her up to her room and got her ready for bed as usual, even though it was only six-thirty p.m. After putting my mom to bed I turned her television to her favorite channel kissed her good night and told her that I'd see her a little later and closed her door behind me, which I never did, I always left her door open, but tonight I did not want her to hear what was about to happen next.

When I got downstairs, Ken was sitting on the couch listening to love songs. I went and stood in front of him, he looked up at me I was really mad I said where the fuck were you last night, you told me that you went to Virginia, he said what are you talking about, I said who the hell were you fucking last night, he said woman you are crazy. I said mother-fucker I want to know the truth I'm tired of your lies. He said I went there by myself and I slept by myself.

I grabbed his shirt and pulled him into the bathroom, he seemed a little scared he had no clue what I was doing. Once we were in the bathroom I asked him to turn to the left and look into the mirror. He said what, I showed him the hickey I said what the fuck is that, and how did it get there if you slept by yourself. He said woman you are crazy I don't know what you are talking about I must have been injured without even knowing it. I said the only way you could have gotten this is by having some bitch suck on your fucking neck, you whore. I hate you and I don't want to ever see you again. I was crying and screaming to the top of my voice, he kept trying to hold me and calm me down, I told him to get his filthy fucking hands off of me. He swore that he was alone and nothing of that sort happened. I stopped talking to him. I decided that I was not going to have anything to do with him. I was doing the laundry a few days later, as I emptied the pockets before putting Ken's pants into the washing machine, I found a receipt, from a restaurant in Virginia dated the same night Ken was there. The receipt had the number of the table listed on it. It also listed that the number of guests were two. I immediately confronted him with this, he said that he was so hungry, that he ordered two dinners, one he ate there and the other he took with him to the hotel. I said no, the receipt has the amount of guests at table # 7 listed as two.

A few days later Ken said I've been thinking about something a lot, I said what is it, he said that I should call Rebecca and offer her to come over if she wanted to visit her grandmother, because since she came home from the rehab Rebecca had not been able to see her. I asked him how come he had this sudden compassion for Rebecca, because I knew that he was still hurting from all the things she had put him through. He said that he had been thinking about it, and even though he was still hurt, he felt that she should be able to see her grandmother and vise-versa. I felt his forehead to check whether he had a temperature or not. I asked him why was he trying to be nice to me, and if he was doing this out of guilt. He said that he had nothing to be guilty of, because he didn't do anything wrong. I asked him to explain the hickey on his neck, he said that he was moving carpets, and it must have rubbed against his neck. I said that hickey was no carpet bruise. He knew that making the offer to have Rebecca come and visit her grandmother would appeal to me and possibly calm me down. I fell for the bait. It was just before thanksgiving I called Rebecca and invited her over to have dinner with us. She accepted, it seemed as though she was happy to be coming over. Ken went over to the city to be with his family. Rebecca spent some time with her grandmother her visit was quiet and uneventful.

Christmas was approaching, and I knew this would be very different for me. I always had very large Christmas dinners with all of our family members present, but this year I was not feeling it. I didn't want to be around any one in a festive way, I was too depressed. I invited Rebecca for breakfast on Christmas day, and she accepted. We exchanged gifts, but there was not the usual festive feeling in our household. Rebecca did not seem to be very happy where she was staying, but I avoided any conversation which led in that direction. Later that night, Rebecca called to say she wasn't feeling well she had thrown up and her aunt wasn't helping her, and she told her to grow up and stop being a baby. She asked me to go over to her aunt's house to see about her, I told her that was not possible, I couldn't leave her grandmother alone, it was snowing, and it was a far distance from me. Rebecca called her cousin Melba, her aunt's daughter. She went over and brought Rebecca ginger ale and Pepto-Bismol and helped her into bed. The following day she said her aunt was upset with her because she had someone from the outside come over to help her out, when she should have handled the situation herself apparently they had some words over this.

Rebecca paid a visit to my sister Valarie she told her she was sick the night before and her aunt Trina the one she was staying with refused to assist her when she needed some help. My sister told me Rebecca was very unhappy and she should come back home. I told her Rebecca had burnt too many bridges when she left, and I didn't think it would be a good idea for her to come back, but I would speak to Ken about it. I asked Ken how he felt about Rebecca coming back home, he said she is your daughter, and I can't stop you from bringing her back, but if she does come back I will not be staying here. He said it very mater of factly, and I thought with time, he might reconsider and change his mind. Rebecca and I spoke about the issues which had created those problems in the first place, and she promised she would be respectful to both of us if she was allowed to come back home. I told her I would allow her to stay here for three months that should be enough time to save up some money to get her own apartment. She agreed to all of this, I reminded her that she couldn't live in the same house with Ken while she had a restraining order against him she would have to go back to court and have it removed she jumped up and said hell no. I reminded her that legally she couldn't live in the same house with him. She said she had to make some phone calls, Rebecca called me back and said she would remove the restraining order because she wanted to come back home.

When Rebecca moved back in, Ken packed his bag and told me that he was leaving. I asked him why he was leaving, he said I told you I would not stay in the same house with her and you still brought her here. I said I didn't think you were really serious, I pleaded with him not to go, he said I can't stay, and then he left. I was devastated. I cried a lot that night. I called him several times, and each time he told me the same thing, he said I cannot live in the same house with Rebecca, I don't want any problems. The following week was hell Ken stayed away he said he was staying by his sister Kristy. Rebecca was very quiet, not causing any problems, but she still didn't want me to tell her what she should do. She had a job interview I told her she should put in several job applications and not just one. This made her very angry she said she wasn't listening to me, I said listen to this with or without a job you will be out of here by the end of March, it was the middle of January. I told her I was tired of the whole thing, I needed some peace in my life, and it was time I took care of me. She called me selfish saying she would leave before the end of March. She said I used her to remove the restraining order from my man and now I want her out. She also said I was the one who asked her to come back. She brought up past incidences I was so hurt I cried. I called my sister Valarie, and she heard Rebecca talking in the background and asked to speak with her. She told Rebecca she should not speak to me in such a manner and she was being very disrespectful. When Valarie got back on the phone with me, she said Rebecca needed to get out of there before the situation got out of control. She told me she would call our youngest brother David and speak with him and his wife and ask them to take her in until she could get out on her own. Rebecca asked to stay until she had her interview which was two days away, I agreed then she asked to stay until the end of March. I explained to her there was too much tension around the home, and it would be better for everyone involved if she left as planned. I came home early from work on Thursday, and instead of waiting for the weekend, I helped Rebecca pack and accompanied to my brother's house.

I picked Ken up from one of his friend's house and we went to dinner, it had been a while since we had gone out together, and this seemed a little strained. I looked up at him and he was looking at me with a smile on his face. It started to snow. Ken told me that one of his friend's had invited us to a house party on Saturday. I didn't respond, because I really didn't feel like being around anyone, pretending that I was happy and that everything was fine. I knew that Ken was talking to his family and friends about what was happening, I knew I wouldn't feel comfortable around his friends, so I just nodded.

Saturday morning I got up and was preparing to take Wilma my mom's care taker to the hair stylist, she was covering for her friend Della who had some family emergency to take care of. She had decided she would not go home that weekend and asked me to drop her off to get her hair done. Ken told me he had a mandatory meeting at eight o'clock. I told Wilma to reschedule her appointment for a later time.

On returning from his meeting, he offered to take Wilma to her appointment, but I insisted since I had promised to meet Rebecca and help her to get the remainder of her belongings from her aunt Trina. Ken stayed with my mother, I would have taken her, but it was much too cold. Rebecca had a lot more things than I thought, and it took much longer than planned. While I was putting the things into the jeep, Ken called and asked what was taking me so long, he said he had to go to work, and I was holding him up. I said you never mentioned anything about working today, because if you did I would have made other arrangements. I told him I would be home in about half an hour. He kept calling me every ten minutes yelling and screaming at me. I stopped answering my phone he was making me very upset. I took Rebecca's belongings to my brother's house and left. He called again, I was on the Garden State Parkway he said that the guys were waiting and he had to leave. I told him to go ahead and leave I had left my mom alone already for short periods of time.

When I got home my mom was sitting in her chair, she was fine. When Ken came home he was yelling he told me he had to work, and I was putting my daughter in front of him, and he was going to do whatever it was he had to do. I reminded him he never told me he had to work all he said was he had to attend a mandatory meeting. I said if I knew you had to work, I would have made other arrangements. He continued to argue, I decided I wouldn't argue with him anymore, because I did not want to upset my mother. I told him he had tendencies of a pathological liar. Just then Wilma called and said she was ready to be picked up, I was too upset to get

131

her, I asked him to please go and get her and he did. When Wilma came in I asked her what Ken said about him having to work today, she said nothing and I said thank you very much.

Rebecca called she needed a pair of gloves she said she was at the storage putting things away and her hands were freezing. I told her I had gloves and she could come and get it. When she got there I met her downstairs with the gloves, she said she had to use the bathroom, and she wanted to say hello to her granny. I allowed her to go in to use the bathroom and see her granny. After that she wanted to go upstairs, and I told her there was no reason for her to go upstairs. She insisted she still had some things upstairs I said you don't and I don't want you going up there. She started mouthing off as usual, saying she was going to put the restraining order back against Ken. I told her to do whatever she felt was necessary, and this was the same reason why I didn't want her coming here too often, because every time she showed up she created drama.

Ken got dressed for the party he asked me if I was going I said no. He didn't respond. I guess that was the reason he came up with the lie about having to work earlier, and starting an argument with me, to make me mad so I wouldn't want to go with him. I had already decided I wasn't going there was no need to create a scene. He left for his party, this was around five p.m. A little while later Rebecca called, insisting she had left something I told her to come and get it this turned out to be a small bottle of nail glue. She started mouthing off that she can't understand how women can have men control them this way, and in the same breath she was asking me for gas money I gave it to her and told her she should get a job. After she left I went upstairs feeling sorry for myself and the problems I seemed to be having. I reminded myself I had created most of these problems by allowing Rebecca to come back home after all the problems she had created over the summer. On the other hand she is my only child and despite all of her shortcomings I still love and want the very best for her.

My sister in law called and asked how I was doing she said Rebecca told her I seemed to be uneasy, I admitted I was. We spoke for a very long time and she told me all of the things Rebecca had told her. She had only been there for two days, and she had told her aunt her version of the events over the summer. She also told me Rebecca was very convincing. Ken did not come home that night, neither did he call.

When I woke up the next morning, I told myself I'm not going to cry any more, and I was going to pull myself together. I've always been very strong and independent and I needed to get my life back in order. I was done putting up with bull shit from any one. We had breakfast, and I asked Wilma if she had any plans for the day, she said no and I asked her if she would stay with my mom, she said it was ok. I showered got dressed checked the train schedule and took a cab to the train station, where I boarded the train to an undisclosed location. I spent the entire day out of the house, it felt good to be out, I was trying to clear my head and decide what I needed to do about my situation. I never once called home to check on my mom, I figured that if Wilma needed me, she would call me on my cell.

I returned home at eight-thirty that night, when I got there Ken was on the phone, I said hello and kept walking. I went straight to my mom's room I checked her blood sugar and gave her insulin and other medications. I sat and chatted with her for a while asking her how her day was. I went to my room changed and got into bed. Neither one of us said anything to the other. As the saying goes let the games begin, well I'm telling you they have just begun, because from this day on every time he steps out I'm stepping out also. I'm not going to sit back and be disrespected by him or anyone else. I'm taking charge of my life again, no more feeling sorry for myself. The following week we seldom spoke to each other.

Rebecca came by to visit, and I told her from now on she had to call before coming over, because I didn't want her there when Ken was at home. I was afraid she would try to create more problems. One night Ken climbed on top of me, he wanted to have sex this was after not having any intimacy for more than one month. I pushed him off of me and sat up in bed. He asked me what was wrong, I said everything. I told him about himself staying out all night and not even calling. He told me I could call his friends and they would verify he had been with them all the time. I said I'm not married to your friends I don't need verification from any of them. I told him I was tired of his excuses and as far as I was concerned this marriage was over. He didn't think he had done anything wrong. I said put yourself in my place, how would you feel if I was the one who was stepping out every weekend and leaving you at home. How did you feel the other day when you came home and I wasn't here? There was a long pause before he responded, and when he did he apologized for not being as supportive as he should have been.

I was beginning to have problems with the care giver she wasn't showing up on time which was causing me to call out of work at the last minute this was putting my job in jeopardy. I decided it was time to look for someone else to care for my mom. My sister Valarie told me she knew someone who might be interested in the job, I told her to have the woman call me.

Ken and I were out having dinner when my manager called to notify me we were going to have a late start the following day. She asked me to go into work later than usual. She had left a message with my mom's care giver, but she felt the message would not be relayed to me. When we arrived home I asked Wilma if there were any messages, she said my manager had called, I asked her if there were any other messages and she said no. Later on Valarie called, she said the woman she referred to take care of my mom called to say she wanted to take the job, but she was told the position had been filled. Wilma told her the position was filled, she said she was hired for the job. I couldn't believe she was so bold, she knew I was planning to get rid of her, she was very unreliable and dishonest I couldn't trust her. I kept my conversations with her to a minimum, I had decided when she left to go home on the weekend, she would not be returning. She knew her time was running out and she didn't go home for the weekend. The following Friday as she was preparing to leave, I told her she shouldn't return on Sunday, because I would be taking care of my mom until other arrangements were made. She said so you'll call me when you are ready for me to return to work. I said you have made things very difficult for me you call at the last moment to say you'll be late or you can't make it in for a day or two. This creates difficult situations for me I have no other choice but to stay at home with my mom. I have a job, and whenever you call out at the last moment, I also have to call out at the last moment. Your behavior is affecting my job and my reputation in a negative way, and because of this I have to find someone who is reliable. She lived in Brooklyn and somehow she felt it was our responsibility to take her home every Friday and pick her up on Sunday to bring her back to work. She called one Sunday evening and said her knee was hurting, and if Kendrick didn't pick her up she wouldn't be coming to work. I told her it was her responsibility to get back and forth to work and Ken would not be picking her up. A few days later she called and apologized for her behavior and asked if she could have her job back. I said Wilma I'm very sorry but I need someone who I can depend on to be here with my mom while I'm at work. She started to cry and promised she would be more responsible, but it was too late, she had already been replaced.

Drina the new care giver started work on Monday. She was the fourth care giver my mom had since she came home from the hospital one and a half years ago. She indeed turned out to be the best of all of them. She was very good with my mom, she was pleasant and peaceful and my mom liked her very much. My mom was happy to see Wilma go. My mom's appetite was very poor, her blood sugar was becoming uncontrollable, she hardly ate and when we tried to feed her, she became very upset with us and refused to eat.

Drina the new care taker started work that Monday. This was the fourth care taker within the one and a half years since my mom had come back home. She indeed turned out to be the best, she was very good with my mom, she was a very pleasant and peaceful person and my mom liked her very much. My mom's blood sugar was becoming uncontrollable, her appetite had become very poor, she hardly ate, and when I tried to feed her she refused.

I called up her doctor, and he told me that I should bring her to the hospital's ER. She was so weak that Ken carried her in his arms down the stairs. We took her to the hospital I used to work at, where I knew most of the doctors and nurses. I had worked there for twenty years, and I knew that she would get excellent care. Her medical doctor practiced there also. I called our priest and told her that my mom was hospitalized again, she visited blessed her and gave her holy communion. I was standing outside my mom's room talking to the priest and all of a sudden I became so overwhelmed, I started crying. She offered some words of comfort.

My mom's blood sugar was regulated with insulin injections four times daily. Discharge plans were made for her to return home with the same insulin schedule. I voiced my concerns to her Doctor I told him it would be difficult for her to receive her injections four times daily while monitoring her blood sugar, since I worked full time and her care giver was not certified to care for her at this level. He suggested she should go to a nursing home at least for a while where she would receive the continuous care she required, and when she got stronger she would return home. She was transferred to a nursing home which was located within close proximity to my place of employment. Every day at lunch time I visited her to assist with her meals. Her appetite was still poor she was not eating enough to sustain life. We discussed putting in a feeding tube, but she refused she made it absolutely clear she did not want to have the tube back in her stomach. We gave her as much as she would take orally.

One day as I was feeding her in the lunch room, a resident who was sitting at the table across from her started to choke on his food. There was one assistant circulating in the lunch room, and when she saw this instead of coming to his aid, she ran out of the room. I assumed she went to get help. I looked over at him, he was struggling to catch his breath and his color was turning purple. I ran over to his table, got behind him and did the Heimlich maneuver. The chunk of food he had ingested flew out of his mouth and his color returned to normal. I returned to my mom's table to assist with her meal. Shortly after the assistant came back into the room with another person, she looked over at the resident's table and saw that he was ok they both left no one asked any questions. Apparently she didn't know what to do, so she ran for help. When I returned to work, I told my friend Jessica what I had just experienced. She asked me if I reported the matter and I said no. Jessica said you are crazy not to, I told her I didn't want to get the assistant into trouble. She reminded me it could have been my mother who was choking, and I would want the staff member who was assigned to her care to be competent. I said you are absolutely right I went straight to the phone and called the nursing home. I asked to speak to the director of nurses I told her my name and that I'm a registered nurse, and the incident I observed while I was feeding my mother. I suggested her entire staff should be BLS certified and if they were already certified maybe a refresher course would be helpful to those who didn't know how to help a choking victim.

She apologized and thanked me, and promised she would look into the matter. A few days later as I visited my mom, I heard an announcement that BLS class was about to begin in the conference room. I was very pleased to know the nursing director had taken immediate action to rectify the problem.

It was now springtime, Ken and I had made prior arrangements to go to Georgetown for two weeks. His sister Kristy had a beautiful house built in Georgetown, and she planned a grand open house in April of 2004. All of his immediately family members were going and we were all looking forward to this trip. As the time got closer I started to have second thoughts about going, mainly because of my mom's condition. I didn't want to be so far away from her for an extended period of time. I voiced my concerns to Ken, and he said he was going and maybe I should go for one week instead of two. I thought about his suggestion, but in the end I decided it would not be a wise decision for me to leave her at this time. I immediately called up the ticket agent and put my ticket on hold. I felt as though a weight had been lifted off of my shoulders after I cancelled my trip, the guilty feeling I was experiencing was gone. Ken left as planned for his trip to Georgetown.

It was my day off and I had decided I would sleep in late then get ready for my appointment at two in the afternoon. I was not looking forward to this appointment, but I felt it was necessary. I was going to make the arrangements for my mom's funeral so when the time arose, everything would be in place. My friend Jessica had planned on meeting me there she felt I shouldn't be undertaking this task alone. My phone rang at six a.m. on April 20th. When I answered it was the nursing home, and the nurse suggested I come in as soon as possible because my mom's respirations had changed. I jumped out of bed got ready and left. On my way there I called Adrian but his phone went right into voice mail. I called Rebecca and she said she would meet me at the nursing home.

My brother and I were there the night before visiting our mom. She was sitting up in bed smiling and taking sips of water and liquid nutrients. I thought she was getting better and would soon be home with us. When I arrived my mother was experiencing Cheyne-Stokes respirations. I held her hands and called her name, I knew she heard me, because her eyelids moved in an attempt to open her eyes but she just didn't have the strength to do so. Rebecca arrived shortly after, we both held her hands and talked to her but she was not trying to respond anymore. Her breathing was becoming more labored we told her we loved her and what a wonderful person she is and we were not going to leave her bedside. I whispered to Rebecca granny is leaving us she started to cry and said I shouldn't say that. I kept trying to reach Adrian, but he never answered his phone. I looked at my mom as she took her last breath and I said to Rebecca this is it granny is gone she started bawling, and I tried to comfort her. My mom died a peaceful death there was no struggle at all. She died two weeks before her eighty-fourth birthday.

I notified the nursing staff my mom had taken her last breath. Her nurse came into the room with her stethoscope and listened to her chest for breath sounds then she checked for pulses. Neither one was present. After she was officially pronounced dead, the funeral home was notified. When the undertaker arrived, I left the room. I couldn't stand to watch as they put my mother into a body bag this was too final for me.

I couldn't cry I had no tears left I had cried so much during her illness and all of the struggles I had been going through with my family. I called the priest when I had first gotten there and asked her to come. When she arrived she blessed my mom and offered comforting words to us. I notified my manager my mom had passed, and she immediately sent two of my co-workers over to be with me, she said I shouldn't be alone at this time. I called Ken's brother Ray and asked him to call Ken and notify him my mother had passed. Ken arrived home two days before the burial. I was so thankful I did not make the trip to Georgetown. I never would have forgiven myself for not being there for my mom during her final moments. I made all of the necessary arrangements, and all of our family and friends came from far and near. My mom was laid to rest on April 24th 2004.